D1097501

OFF THE WALL

Also by Camilla Reghelini Rivers
in the Lorimer Sports Stories series

Red-Line Blues
Shut-Out!

OFF THE WALL

Camilla Reghelini Rivers

James Lorimer & Company Ltd., Publishers
Toronto

James Lorimer & Company Ltd., Publishers acknowledges the support of the
Ontario Arts Council. We acknowledge the financial support of the Government
of Canada through the Canada Book Fund for our publishing activities. We
acknowledge the support of the Canada Council for the Arts which last year
invested $20.1 million in writing and publishing throughout Canada. We
acknowledge the Government of Ontario through the Ontario Media
Development Corporation's Ontario Book Initiative.

Cover Image: iStockphoto

Library and Archives Canada Cataloguing in Publication

Rivers, Camilla Reghelini
    Off the wall / Camilla Reghelini Rivers.

(Sports stories)
Issued also in an electronic format.
ISBN 978-1-55277-841-8

       I. Title. II. Series: Sports stories (Toronto, Ont.)

PS8585.I8776O43 2011   jC813'.6   C2011-902030-0

James Lorimer & Company Ltd.,	Distributed in the United States by:
Publishers	Orca Book Publishers
317 Adelaide St. West	P.O. Box 468
Suite 1002	Custer, WA USA
Toronto, ON, Canada	98240-0468
M5V 1P9	
www.lorimer.ca	

Printed and bound in Canada.
Manufactured by Friesens Corporation in Altona, Manitoba, Canada in July 2011
Job # 66773

To Damien, Tristan, and Rhiannon
and all the Vern Hieberts who have coached them
like: Ron, Mia, Bob, Pam, Dave, Greg, Charles K.,
Rudolph, Terry, Karen, and Willy

CONTENTS

1 FOOD FOR THOUGHT

Average. Everything about me is average, I thought, glaring at my own image. My looks. My abilities. Let's face it, that's what I am. The reflection staring back at me from the mirror is drab. My hair's mousy and straight. My eyes? Good old brown. I'm sure my parents had a hunch when they picked the name Jane for me. Get it? Plain Jane. I'm so grateful that it's not my first name and that my last isn't Brown. Elizabeth Jane Ash — that's my full name. Thank goodness everyone calls me Lizzie.

Sighing, I put the brush down and thumped downstairs to the kitchen.

"Lizzie, stop taking your anger out on the stairs."

"I'm not angry, just worried," I mumbled.

"About the bus? Trust me, Lizzie, it's easy. It's only one bus and the stop's right across the street." Mom reached over and brushed a lock of hair off my face.

"But, *Mom* —"

"I'd drop you off if I could, but I can't be late for

work today. There's a client coming in." She took my chin in her hand. "It's hard growing up. Those first steps are scary, but you can do it, believe me."

"Yeah, but how'll I know where to get off?" I whined. I'd never taken a bus before.

"You can't miss it. Get off at the gas station, by the shopping centre." She brushed my forehead with her lips and waved goodbye.

I let out a sigh and wallowed in my mixed emotions.

Grade seven. Junior high. I had been looking forward to it so much since orientation day. It was the same school as last year, but we had our own wing and teachers. Teachers who didn't know me or Shelby, so they couldn't constantly remind me how exceptional she was.

Shelby's my sister. She isn't anything like me, though. She's cute and elflike, with curly blond hair and a heart-shaped face. She's a natural — good at everything. Unfortunately, she has no interests of her own, so she copies whatever I do and does it better.

For the most part I don't mind, even though she is two years younger, because she's a good kid. She never sticks to anything anyway, so we aren't often competing. It's just that for the last four years I've been living in her shadow. When people are really talented the world trips over itself to help them succeed. I wish that average people who work hard, like me, could be respected for their achievements too. But as if that's ever going to happen. So a world of my own is the next best thing.

Finally I had the chance to start fresh. Junior high's a wonderful world of science labs, band rooms, and lockers. Students unlucky enough to have gone to schools that end with grade six come to our school.

My locker partner, Pam, was one of these. She wasn't a stranger, though, because we'd played soccer together for the last three years. She's a bit of a motormouth, but we hit it off right away. I was so glad she was in my class, since my best friend had moved away that summer.

The challenges started right off the bat. The first day of school was a Tuesday. Everything would have been fine if it weren't for that. Each Tuesday morning we were supposed to go to Shops — that's what we called home ec and industrial arts. We'd be rotating through Foods, Clothing and Textiles, Woods, and Graphics. Unfortunately, there were more students than lab spaces at Paddington and we would have to take some of our sections at other schools. My first rotation was scheduled at one of these. Lucky me.

So there I was, feeling sorry for myself. I waited at the bus stop, a bundle of nerves. What if I got on the wrong bus? Did I have the right fare? I counted my change for the umpteenth time — a dollar eighty-five in quarters, nickels, and dimes. Yes.

When the bus pulled up, I checked the number twice.

"Hey, kid. Getting on or not? Come on, come on,

I don't have all day."

Maybe I didn't climb on fast enough because the driver pulled out with a jerk. I stumbled down the aisle and almost landed on someone. Grabbing the pole, I steadied myself. My eyes rose from the lap I'd just missed and connected with the deepest blue eyes I'd ever seen on someone my age. My face reddened.

"Climb on up, *shweetheart*." He patted his thighs.

Instantly his twinkling eyes and smiling face lost all their charm.

"You wish," I sneered and searched for a seat.

"Lizzie. Over here."

Pam. A safe place. I made my way over and dropped into the empty space.

"Hi. Are you going to Foods? Mine are at Darwin. I don't really know where that is," she said.

"Yeah. I'm going there too. Mom says it's easy to find."

Pam was her usual chatty self. "Are you, like, still sticking with indoor soccer this year?"

"Are you kidding? What kind of question is that?" Soccer is my sport. From the first time I tried it, I loved it.

"I'm staying with indoor soccer, too, but some of the girls from last year aren't. They're going to try out for the school teams," said Pam.

"Too bad for them. Vern's coaching so it'll be great."

"I hate waiting for it to start. October's such a long way off, y'know? Hey look." Pam pointed to the front of the bus.

A number of kids that looked our age were standing up, waiting to get off.

"Do you figure this is our stop? It's gotta be, don't you think?" Pam asked.

"I don't know. My mom said to get off at the gas station by the shopping centre."

"Look, here's a strip mall. And there's a gas bar across the street. How bang-on can you get? Let's go, 'kay?"

I stood up reluctantly. "I don't know, Pam. I think she meant the Saint Vital Centre."

"Then why are all these kids getting off here? And, like, how many gas stations by strip malls would have a school nearby?"

She had a point there. I chased after her.

"See ya, cupcake," blue-eyes called after us as we passed his seat.

Cupcake? It sounded like something my grandfather would say. What time warp had that toad stepped through?

Pam giggled and blushed but I stayed cool and ignored him.

We followed the others and they led us right to the wrong school. Minetonka.

"Oh, great."

"Sorry, sorry, Lizzie. Like, how was I supposed to know? Ooh, we're going to be late!" She twirled a lock of her blond hair around her finger.

"Let's go to the office and ask someone," I suggested.

The office was filled with people trying to get the secretary's attention. By the time it was our turn, the buzzer had gone already.

"It could be worse," she told us. "Darwin's just a few blocks away. Go down Minetonka Street. Hang a right at Riel. It's about a block up."

That sounded easy enough. We took off down the sidewalk. At Riel we turned right, as instructed. A block later we hit Metz. There was no school, only houses on all four corners and down the street in both directions.

"Maybe she meant left? Like, y'know, people say right when they really mean left," Pam said.

We changed directions and passed Minetonka Street again.

"Oh, look. There's lots of trees behind those houses. It's just gotta be the schoolyard," Pam said.

Wrong again, it was only a stupid park.

"This is crazy. I'm going to ask someone."

Two driveways down, a lady was getting into her car.

"Excuse me," I called. "Can you help us? We're supposed to go to Darwin School for Foods but we're lost. Can you give —"

"Some nerve," she cut me off. "What do you take me for? A taxi service? Spoiled teenagers." She slammed the car door, honked the horn, and squealed out of the driveway.

Pam and I looked at each other and burst out

laughing.

"Boy, was that weird," Pam said.

"Yeah. I was just going to ask her for directions."

"Don't worry about her. She's just a crabby lady," a raspy little voice said — startling both of us.

A small boy was standing in the next yard. In each hand he carried a loaded shopping bag of school supplies.

"You're looking for Darwin? I'm going there. This way." He turned in the direction we had first come and ran — or, should I say, waddled down the street, because of his load.

Catching up, Pam and I each grabbed a bag from him and hustled.

Two blocks from Minetonka, we hit Darwin Street and there it was — Darwin School.

"You'll need a late slip. I get lots of them. Come on, I'll show you the office."

We followed him as he confidently walked into the building.

"Hi, Mrs. R. I brought friends," he said.

"Hi, Mark." The secretary handed him a piece of paper. "You hurry along, I'll take care of the girls. Shops?" she asked.

We nodded.

"Down that hall and to the left," she said, pointing.

Relieved, I knocked on the door labelled "Foods Lab."

"Late on the first day." The teacher sighed and ran

her hand through her grey wiry hair. "First impressions are lasting impressions. Go take a seat."

I looked around the room and saw lots of familiar faces. I headed for two empty spaces where Pam and I could sit together.

"Well, if it isn't cupcake and Pam."

Great — the jerk from the bus — how could I have missed that head of orangey-red hair?

"You know that creep?" I whispered to Pam.

"He isn't a creep. He's so cool. Don't you think he's hot?"

I begrudgingly admitted to myself that he was good-looking, but he was also a Grade-A pest.

"Brock was in my class last year at Penner Elementary," Pam continued. "We are *so* lucky he's in our homeroom at Paddington too."

"Pam! How come you never figured out we had the wrong stop? Didn't you wonder why he wasn't getting off?"

"Heck no. I figured his Shops were, like, somewhere else. Our whole class isn't in the same course, y'know."

Just great. What a perfectly awful day this had started out to be. I prayed that the rest of junior high wasn't going to be the same.

2 CUPCAKE AND BROCK-O-LI

"Oops. Sorry." Brock smiled and winked at me as he dodged down the hall.

"Watch it." I rubbed my shoulder where it had bashed into the locker. "I swear he bumped me on purpose."

"Oh, don't be paranoid, Lizzie. It's, like, packed in here." Pam stuffed her backpack into the locker.

She was right. The hall was so crammed that a sardine would've felt at home, but I still had my suspicions. For the last three weeks, whenever I turned around, Brock was there.

I didn't wait for Pam, but turned and elbowed my way to the classroom. I wanted my pick of seats.

"I'll save you a spot," I called to her.

I went to the front, plunked myself down in the chair and placed a book on the desk behind me.

The room started to fill.

"What's the rush?" Pam handed back my book. "Aw, Lizzie, do we have to sit here? You know Mr. Henchel's

17

going to, like, ask me questions if he sees me. There's room in the ba—"

"Look, if you want to sit back there, you can. But I'm not moving." I figured I'd shake Brock by sitting in the first row — he seemed to be the *sit in the back and clown around* type.

Rats. Before Pam could seat herself, he waltzed up and plopped himself down.

"This place isn't taken — is it, Pam?" He gave her a mega-smile.

I glared at Pam but she ignored me.

"It's free, Brock. I was going to sit in the back ... but I think I'll just sit here." She dropped her butt onto the seat behind him, then grinned and batted her eyelashes, blushing beet red.

"Well, cupcake? Get your math homework done? Can I copy it?" His blue eyes twinkled.

"Like I'd ever let you copy my stuff." I turned and faced the front. If he "cupcakes" me again he's going to be sorry, I thought.

We started math class by going over the assignment from the day before. Mr. Henchel randomly asked kids for answers. If you had a problem wrong, he'd explain the stuff again using that question as the example.

Getting the answer right was actually worse. He made you go to the front and show how you got it.

"If you can teach something, it means you understand it," he'd say.

Ask Brock a question, I prayed. The twirp was leaning back, slouched down in his seat — his open binder held in place by his gut and the edge of the desk. So self-assured that I wanted him taken down a peg.

My prayer was answered.

"X equals three," he said.

Whoa, cocky or what? Henchel was going to find out he hadn't done his homework, anyway.

"Correct. Now show us how you got that." Mr. Henchel smiled at him.

All right, truth time, I thought.

Sure of himself as ever — he slowly sat up, snapped open his binder, and took out a page. He then proceeded to copy the correct method off his sheet and explain clearly what he did.

He smirked as he passed me on the way back to his seat.

"Jerk," I said, glaring at him.

"What did I do?" he asked innocently.

"You're a liar."

"Am not."

"Are too. You said you didn't do your homework."

"Never did. Why would I say that? I always do my homework." He tried to look hurt but the corners of his lips kept turning up.

"You asked to copy mine. That's the same thing."

"No it's not. Just wanted to see if you would lend me stuff." He broke into a smile.

"You could've asked for a pen."

"Why would I ask for a pen? I don't need your pen. See, I have my own." His smile widened into a grin.

"You didn't need my home— oh, forget it." He was just messing with my mind.

"Care to share your wisdom with the class?" Mr. Henchel stared at me.

Me? Why me? The creep was whispering just as much.

"I … I … "

"She just wanted to know that last step, sir."

"Next time, Lizzie, ask out loud — so we can all benefit. Now, where were we? Ah yes. Question thirteen."

"What? No 'Thank you'?" Brock whispered to my back.

"Shut up," I whispered back through clenched teeth.

"For heaven's sake, I was only trying to help."

"Well, don't. Just — leave — me — alone."

"Lizzie. Brock. Next time, you're in the hall." Mr. Henchel spoke softly but you could tell he was mad.

One thing I knew for sure — I wasn't going to let some bigmouth get me thrown out of class. I hid my red face with my binder and tried to concentrate, but Brock was lightly tapping his pen on a book. It was driving me crazy.

Everything about him was starting to bug me — not just his smart mouth, but the way he moved and the way he sat. Even the stupid smile on his freckled face got on my nerves. As far as I was concerned, I wanted to stay as far away from him as I could get.

Next class change I altered my strategy. Instead of being the first one into the room, I decided to be the last. Surely there would be an empty seat far away from the dork. I lingered by the water fountain to make sure Brock and his friends had gone in, then I followed behind the last group of kids.

Pam waved her arms to get my attention. "Lizzie. I saved you a seat."

She had, too — right beside the idiot.

I hadn't counted on Pam's crush. She looked so pleased with herself. How could I hurt her feelings? I took the place she had reserved, but I knew we were due for a nice long talk. Lunchtime would do nicely.

★ ★ ★

"We can't sit by that jerk again." I scowled at my tuna sandwich.

"But, Lizzie, why? He's, like, so funny. This morning in math, wasn't that hilarious? He sure got you. These last few weeks have been great. So why can't we sit near him?" She flicked a strand of chin-length hair off her face.

"He nearly got me thrown out of class, for heaven's sake. You might have thought it was funny, but I didn't."

"Oh, Lizzie. He didn't mean to. It's just his way of kidding around."

"He can keep his jokes to himself. They're driving me nuts."

"But...but you don't understand. I've had this mega-crush on him since last year. He's funny and smart and good-looking, too. All the girls want him."

Not me, I thought. I've got him figured out. Popular boys, like Brock, used girls like us for one thing — the brunt of their jokes.

"He's never even looked my way before," she continued. "He's finally noticing me. Why would I ignore him now?"

"Look, Pam, that jerk has it in for me. I don't want to sit near him. Okay?"

Pam reached over and grabbed my wrist. "Can't you, like, be a friend? Do it for me. *Please.*"

I wasn't going to get anywhere. Her big blue doe eyes made that clear.

"All right," I said. "We can sit near him. But this is the deal — I don't want him in front of me, to the side of me, or behind me. You had better be between us at all times — or else."

"Got ya. Thank you, thank you!" She jumped up and down.

"Pam, sit. You're making a scene." The lunch ladies were looking at us.

"Okay, okay. You won't be sorry, Lizzie, I promise.

By the way, don't you want that sandwich? I'll have it."

I guess I was still scowling at my lunch. "Forget it. Tuna's my favourite."

I took a big bite. Mom had made it just the way I liked it, with onions and celery and lots of mayo. I closed my eyes to savour the taste.

"Waiting for a kiss, cupcake?"

Oh, great, speak of the devil. There he was standing in front of me with his lips puckered.

His friends and Pam giggled.

I don't know if it was the onions and celery — those veggies — that inspired me, but I groaned and blurted out, "Definitely not from the Brock-o-li."

For a minute there was silence, then his friends got it. They laughed even louder. Potato-head himself wasn't amused. He turned and shuffled away.

One point for Lizzie, I thought.

"Oh no. I think you, like, hurt his feelings."

"Vegetables don't have feelings."

"You sure can be mean, y'know, Lizzie."

"Get real, Pam. He's been calling me cupcake from day one. You didn't mind that."

"Well … that's different. A cupcake's a good thing but people, like, hate broccoli."

"The way I see it, food is food. Anyway, I like broccoli."

"So, you were just kidding before? You think Brock's nice, too?"

"Stop being so dense. I — like — the — green stuff. Not the loser, okay?"

"You know what, Lizzie? *You're* the loser." She flounced out of the lunchroom.

"Pam, wait! What did I say?" I ran after her.

"You know how I feel about him and you still keep putting him down."

"I'm sorry, sometimes I don't think before I speak. Friends again?" I reached out and took her hand.

"Friends." She smiled back at me.

"Hey, look, Jen brought a soccer ball. Let's go." I dashed across the schoolyard, glad to have a chance to kick the ball around. For me, the time between the outdoor and indoor seasons always seemed like forever.

After lunch, in Language Arts class, the Brock-o-li kept giving me funny looks. He never said a word to me, but he spoke to Pam in a real friendly way. Maybe he did like her. I didn't care. I was happy to have him off my case — that's all.

3 AW, BEANS!

The sky was pouring buckets when I headed for the bus that Saturday morning. The duck boots and raincoat my mother suggested I wear were so uncool. I had put on my soccer jacket and runners instead. After all, I was in junior high.

I pulled my baseball cap low over my eyes, hoping to protect my face from the driving rain. My hair was still getting wet so I tucked it into my jacket. At the bus stop, I hunched my shoulders and paced, keeping my eyes glued to the sidewalk for fear of stepping into puddles. I never noticed the bus until it pulled up and sprayed me. Feeling like a drowned rat, I climbed the steps.

Mom had offered to drop us off at the movies, but I had insisted on taking transit. I liked my new-found freedom and was afraid that Shelby would ask to tag along if Mom was driving. Now I almost wished I'd taken the ride.

It's hard enough picking out a short person on a

bus at the best of times, but when it's crowded with kids — like it was that day because of the rain — it's near impossible. If Pam hadn't worn her soccer jacket, I don't think I'd have noticed her arm waving. She was sitting near the back, in those sideways seats. Seated beside her was this odd little man. He was wearing a trench coat that looked a bit big for him. His face was hidden by the brim of his old-man hat. You know, the kind your grandpa might wear when he gets dressed up. She was yapping away to him. Too friendly, if you ask me. Man, she can be so dumb sometimes.

"Pam, I hate sitting sideways. Let's move. There's two empty seats in the very back."

The man turned and looked at me. Whoa. It was Mr. Green-trees — Brock — wearing the latest fashions for the homeless.

I know I'd promised to be nicer to him, but I couldn't help myself. I burst out laughing.

"You've got to be kidding. They're not going to let you into an adult movie just because you're dressed like that. You look like a freak. They'll call the cops."

Brock only shrugged but Pam gave me a dirty look — she was really mad.

"You should think before being a jerk, Lizzie. You don't know everything, y'know."

She wouldn't speak to me again. She just talked to the Brock-o-li. When the bus pulled up to the Saint Vital Centre, she pushed her way to the exit. By the time I got off, she was halfway to the mall. Brock wasn't with her. I searched the crowd for him and caught a glimpse of him climbing onto another bus. He wasn't going to the movies. I wondered about Pam's crack regarding not knowing stuff. Maybe Brock was poor or something and his parents made him wear those clothes. No self-respecting twelve-year-old would be caught dead in that outfit otherwise.

Pam wasn't in the foyer of the theater when I got there. Well, if she wants to be like that, I'm not chasing after her, I thought. And I'm sure as heck not sitting through a movie I know I'll hate. Pam had talked me into seeing one of those movies where the main character is *so* dumb and his sidekick is even dumber. She liked slapstick humour. No wonder she thought Brock was funny. I looked at the sign and picked a romance instead.

The bus ride to Foods on Tuesday was totally different because by Sunday we were friends again.

"Okay, class. Settle down. Today we're studying proteins. There are two main sources. Animal products, and pulses and nuts."

"What are pulses?" someone asked.

Ms. Oliver turned to the class. "Anyone?"

"It's beans and lentils and stuff," I said. Mom was

always trying to get us to eat healthy, so she'd cooked some meat-alternative recipes. I hated most of them.

"That's right, Libby. Oh excuse me — Lizzie. Must have beans on my brain. How silly of me." The teacher giggled.

"Libby's Beans? You mean the kind that make you toot? You know ... " Brock put his hand in his armpit to demonstrate.

The class laughed.

"That's enough." Ms. Oliver pursed her lips and stared at Brock.

When we were in our kitchens, Brock asked in a loud voice, "Lizzie's Beans, do you have any salt?"

The whole room heard. After that the other kids did the same. It was — hey, Lizzie's Beans this, or Lizzie's Beans that.

Then Brock started to sing quietly. I could hear him from the next kitchen. "Lizzie's Beans, beans, the musical fruit. The more Lizzie eats, the more she toots."

"Knock it off!" I yelled.

Of course he didn't listen, he just got louder — punctuating each line with an armpit fart.

"Stop that this minute! I won't tolerate disgusting behaviour in my class." Ms. Oliver glared at him.

"Yes, ma'am." The Brock-o-li could sound humble when he wanted to.

He behaved himself the rest of the morning. On

the way back to Paddington he sat and joked with the other boys.

Pam wasn't happy about that. She acted as if it was my fault, but there was no way she could pin anything on me. I hadn't even called him Brock-o-li once. After what had happened on Saturday, I'd played it cool, not wanting to set her off.

When the bus stopped at the school, I didn't get off. I figured there was no point in going to the lunchroom because Pam was sulking. I headed home instead — grateful for the longer lunch breaks on Foods days.

I was glad the first class that afternoon was Band. Our seats were assigned by the instrument we played. I played the clarinet. Pam played the flute. The Brock-o-li played tuba, thank goodness. That section sat in the back of the room.

As we waited for the teacher, you could hear the tuba section playing loudly. Oomp, oomph, pa-oomp-pa-oomph. Soon the percussion section joined in. Then they started singing — they were the only ones without instruments in their mouths. "Lizzie's Beans, the musical fruit. The more she eats, the more she toots."

It was bad enough being bugged by the kids from Foods. Now all the grade sevens in the school would be teasing me. The three classes took band together.

I'd had it. A week of Lizzie's Beans and armpit toots from kids was more than enough for me. This was war. One way or another, the Brock-o-li was going to get it. To heck with Pam's feelings.

After school Brock and his friends were horsing around between the lockers and the door, trying to push each other out into the pouring rain. One of the guys grabbed the Brock-o-li's overstuffed backpack. The old-man hat fell out of the partially open bag. The boy threw it to another, reached in and pulled out the trench coat, and danced around with it. Brock grabbed his things back, put them on and pretended to be a spy. He looked dorky.

"Hey Brock. What an outfit!" I yelled, making sure everyone turned and stared at him. "You might think you're *James Bond* but you look like *Inspector Gadget.*"

Here and there, kids laughed. Some joined in on the razzing.

"Hey, Brockie. Cool clothes."

"Better be careful. Ms. Hothands might mistake you for a new sub and grab a hug," teased a grade-niner.

Ms. Hothands was actually Ms. Horton, the school secretary. Wrinkles and all, she thought she was hot stuff. Jeez, it made you gag to see her in action.

The Brock-o-li didn't say anything. He just tipped his hat and bowed, then hurried out into the rain.

"That was *so* mean." Pam slammed the locker door and raced after him.

Ouch. I guess she hadn't noticed my fingers were there. Otherwise, I'm sure she wouldn't have done that.

When my fingers stopped throbbing, I grabbed my backpack and locked up. I had to hurry to get home before Shelby, because I had the house key.

I'd worried for nothing because Shelby and her friends were still hanging around outside the school.

"Hi, Lizzie. Want to walk with us?"

I hesitated for a moment. Oh, what the heck. I could be walking them home because I *had* to, I thought. No one was going to know differently. Right?

I nodded.

"Where's Pam?" Shelby asked.

"It's raining. She took the bus," I lied. I figured it was none of her business.

Pam and I usually walked home from school together. We lived in the same direction — except her house was much farther. I wished we weren't fighting because I missed listening to her prattle on.

" ... more soup, Lizzie?" My sister's voice filtered through.

"Huh? More soup?"

"No, not soup, silly. Marsupial. Do you know anything about them?"

"Yeah. Some. Why?" I asked.

"We're studying marsupials. Will you help me with my project?"

"Yeah, sure." I finally managed to open the door

after rattling the knob a few times. I swear my key's a dud.

I don't know why Shelby asks me for help; she always does, but in the end she never needs me. Maybe she just likes being in my room, because we've always worked there when I've helped her.

I turned the radio to HOT 103 and we sprawled on my bed. Shelby made notes while I looked at the pictures in her books.

"Jeez, look at this thing — the ugly offspring of a beaver and a duck." I took a bite out of the apple I was munching on.

Shelby didn't even look up. "A platypus. That's the animal I chose. Neat, huh?" Her untouched apple rolled off the pile of books as she grabbed for one of them.

"They lay eggs, you know. Hey . . . I've got an idea. What if I do my project in an egg-shaped, two-layered poster. The top one's a cracked shell. Where it's cracked you open it. The written part is on the bottom layer. What do you think?" She smiled.

"Excellent!" Like I said, she didn't need me. I wished I could come up with cool ideas like that.

"Hi guys. What are you up to? Here, Lizzie. It was in the mail box." Mom tossed the community club's newsletter to me.

"Hi Mom. Thanks. When did you get home? I never heard you come in."

"I just got in." She walked over to my radio and

adjusted the volume. "If you two turned this down, maybe you would hear what's going on in the world around you."

"Oh no, Mom. Indoor soccer sign-ups are today. Come on, let's go." I jumped off the bed and headed for the door.

"Slow down, kiddo. You can sign up on Saturday and next Thursday, too. I'm bushed and I'm not going out in that rain again."

"Aw, *Mom*."

"Sorry, sweetie. I'm putting my feet up for five minutes. Then I've got to get supper going." She fluffed her shoulder-length hair to shake out some of the wetness.

"Please. Pretty please. I'll help make supper."

"Please, Lizzie. I've had a really bad day and I'm in no mood for your antics. And you know helping with supper is your chore. Just like washing dishes is Shelby's."

"What do you want me to do?" I called as I flounced into the kitchen.

"Please make the salad. I'll be right there."

I slammed around the kitchen for about two seconds. Then I calmed down because Mom was right, it really made no difference whether I signed up the first day or not. Patience wasn't one of my virtues. If there was something I really wanted to do, I usually bugged Mom until she caved in.

After supper I phoned Pam to talk soccer.

"Hi Pam. It's Lizzie."

"What do you want?" She was still mad at me.

"I just want to say that I'm sorry," I apologized even though I knew that I hadn't done anything wrong. "Can we be friends again?"

"Not if you keep knocking Brock."

"Look, Pam." I was getting a little ticked myself. "I like you and I want to stay friends, but you've got to admit that Brock picks on me, too ... "

"Okay, okay. Whatever. Let's forget it."

"All right. Truce. Are you signing up for indoor soccer tonight?"

"Yeah. How 'bout you?"

"Naw. Maybe Saturday."

4 PLEASED AS PUNCH

It was Thursday before I could register for division eight indoor soccer. This was my fourth year of playing and I still loved everything about the sport — running, struggling for the ball, the teamwork. But most of all I liked the people — not just the kids, but the coach, too. Vern Hiebert was the best.

Shelby signed up for soccer again too, which was surprising since she'd never done the same thing twice. As it turned out, there were too many ten-year-olds and not enough elevens signed up, so they moved seven of the younger kids up to division nine. Shelby was one of them. I was really happy for her and we made a pact to go and cheer each other on.

Coach Hiebert called a practice as soon as he got the players list. We were to meet at the club on Tuesday at seven o'clock.

That evening Mom and Dad were at meetings and, wouldn't you know it, they both ran late. I decided that this was one of those challenging moments when independent action was required, so I phoned Pam.

"Are you going to soccer?" I asked

"Yeah. What do you think? Duh."

"Could I hitch a ride with you then? Mom and Dad are still at work."

"Yeah, probably, but I'll ask my dad, 'kay?"

I was humming to myself waiting for Pam to get back on the phone when my sister walked into the kitchen. Shelby. I had forgotten all about her. Now what?

"Hey, is there room in the car for one more?" I asked.

"Who else needs a ride?"

"Shelby."

"Why is Shelby coming?"

"I can't leave her home alone. Duh."

"Whatever. We'll be by in fifteen minutes, 'kay?"

"Shelby. Hurry up. We're going to my practice. Do you have homework? Grab your books. Come on. Pam will be here soon." I dashed off a note and attached it with a magnet to the fridge.

I was so proud of myself for solving the problem.

When we arrived at the club gym I got my sister settled in a corner, away from the flying balls. "Finish your work. Then, if you want, you can join us."

I figured it was a safe bet to suggest this because Coach Hiebert was always inviting kids who were hanging around to join our practices.

"Okay, ladies," his voice boomed out. "Gather around, please."

We formed a noisy, chatty semicircle around him, excited to be there. Coach Hiebert waited for a few minutes for us to quiet down — no luck, the noise just got louder.

"Come on, girls. Be quiet for a sec. *Now.*" The last word echoed in the gym as he raised his voice.

Startled, we were silent. Some of the new kids looked worried because he looked intimidating. For starters, he towered over us girls. Thick black eyebrows arched over light brown eyes — scary if he scowled, but he didn't much. The lines in his tanned face were actually etched by smiles.

"Now that I've got your attention, let's get down to business. For those of you who are new to the team, I'm Vern Hiebert. There are a few things I'd like to get straight from the start. Any team I coach is based on three things —"

"Enjoyment, effort, and respect," yelled a number of us who he had coached before.

"Right on." Coach Hiebert high-fived Pam, who was sitting closest to him. "And remember, that goes both ways. For you and me too. I want us to enjoy ourselves. No point in playing if we're not having a good time."

"But … but … sometimes if you're in goal and the other team's racking up the points it's just no fun," said Jen, our goalie from last year.

"I hear ya. But you know I'm not talking about the off-days, Jen. We all have them. I'm looking at the big picture. The season. Practices. The whole experience. Okay?" He looked around and smiled as we nodded. "People put more effort into things when they're having fun. I know I do. And it takes an effort to win. After all, winning is the goal of any sport, isn't it?"

"Thank goodness you're not one of those *it's not if you win or lose, but how you play the game* coaches, like my last year's hockey coach." Alex was big, strong, and aggressive but new to the sport.

"Oh, but I am. What I mean is, the players give it one hundred percent in the *hopes* of winning. But if you've tried your hardest and you don't win — no problem. You can still win and not make it onto the scoreboard at all."

"Huh? What do you mean, Mr. Hiebert?" asked Rosa, Alex's sidekick. She was the opposite of her friend — small and dark.

"What's with this Mr. Hiebert stuff? Call me Vern. What I was trying to say —"

"Vern, can I tell her?" Pam pleaded. We old pros knew what he meant.

"Okay. Go for it."

"Okay. It's like this: if you do your best and you lose the match, you can still be a winner in the *big* game — life — by learning from your mistakes. Right?"

"Yeah, close enough. Anyway, with effort and

respect you can't go wrong. That brings me to practices — we've been assigned Thursdays. Seven-thirty. I'd like all of you to show up, but I realize —" He didn't get to finish because his old players interrupted.

"Life happens."

"Homework comes first."

"There are family obligations."

Recognizing his own words, he chuckled. "Yeah. All of the above. But if you can't make it, please —"

"*Phone*," we chorused.

"You got it," he said.

Another coach might have been upset with us for interrupting, but not Vern. He could take a joke, and he knew we liked him a lot.

"Okay. Let's get to work." He unzipped an enormous black sports bag and started to throw out balls. "Grab a partner. Practise your kicks and passes just to get back into the swing of things."

It was a wild first practice. Balls flew everywhere from rusty shots. We were giggly, silly, and hyper — not yet ready for a serious workout. Coach Hiebert knew it, so he focused on the fun and getting us pumped for the season.

We played hard and were sweaty and tired by the end. It was great.

I flopped down by Pam. Shelby lowered herself beside me. Her blond curls were wet with sweat.

"That was awesome, Lizzie. Can I come again?"

"It's okay with me, but I don't know." I took back my water bottle from her, took a long cold swig, then cooled myself off by dribbling the rest over my head.

"Attention, ladies. I'm going to hand out uniforms. I'll call out the number and the first hand up gets it. Okay?"

I figured I'd take whichever one nobody else wanted as I wasn't into lucky numbers or anything. River Park Community Club had the ugliest uniforms in the whole city. They were so old that they'd faded to the colour of green pea soup. The knit tops had small runs in the fabric and the cotton shorts were stiff and uncomfortable. Last year we'd whined about them.

Vern had laughed and said, "Yeah, you look like a bunch of snakes in the process of shedding your skins."

The team had booed and hissed at his joke. All the club's teams — both boys and girls — are called the Pythons.

Vern looked into the box. "Number ten." He reached in and pulled out the uniform.

We gasped, then started talking all at once.

"New uniforms."

"Awesome."

"Cool."

They were beautiful — a deep, rich green. The top and shorts were of satiny fabrics — almost metallic looking. Woven right into the cloth was a diamond design like snakeskin. Perfect for Pythons.

We were all just sitting there with our jaws hanging, completely in awe. Suddenly I wanted that first uniform. I shot my hand up.

"And the winner is Lizzie." Vern tossed the uniform to me.

I ran my fingers over the shiny black *PYTHONS* printed across the front. The "s" at the end was shaped like a snake — its tail stretched out behind it, underlining the word. There seemed to be power there.

"Nine." The coach pulled out the next one.

Three hands went up instantly. No one was worrying about lucky numbers.

"Alex. I think you were the fastest. Catch."

She held her prize up against her five-foot-six frame. "Hey this won't fit. It's a small," she said as she checked the tag in the neck. "Rosa, I think it'll fit you. Want it?"

Rosa nodded.

"Oops. Guess I should call the size, too. Fourteen, medium."

I hadn't thought to check the size of my uniform. I was afraid to look. I didn't want to give it up, for some strange reason it just felt lucky. I didn't have time to fool around, the box was emptying fast. Slowly, I pulled out the label, medium. It fit. I let the air out of my lungs. Vern rummaged in his bag again. He pulled out the schedules and handed them around. "Here. Make sure you give these to your parents."

"Hey. Where are all the teams?" I looked at the sheet again. Some of last year's teams were missing.

"The Big Three have opted to play up this year. In division seven. They want stronger competition. That leaves division eight wide open," the coach answered.

"Woohoo!"

"All right!"

"Yeah!"

The Big Three were the Hawks, Vics, and Falcons. Their teams were hand-picked, so one of them always won. The rest of us never stood a chance. Now they were gone. Pam grabbed me and we were dancing.

This was going to be an excellent year. I couldn't wait to get home and tell my parents.

★ ★ ★

"Where the heck have you two been?" Mom was standing at the back door, hand on hips, green eyes flashing.

"At ... at soccer practice. You knew it was today. You told me about it." I couldn't understand why she was mad.

"We weren't back from work yet. Your dad and I expected the two of you to be in the house. I told you we had meetings."

"You didn't tell me I had to stay home."

"I didn't think I needed to. I took it for granted that you had enough common sense. What were you thinking? Imagine how we felt finding the house empty, wondering whether the two of you were safe —"

She was making a big deal out of nothing.

"We were safe. At the community club with about six parents and Vern. How much safer could it be?"

"But we didn't know that. We phoned all your friends. They didn't know where you were."

"Pam's dad knew. Mr. Paulsen drove us to the club. You couldn't have called there."

"I did call. There was nobody in."

"But that's not my fault." Of course she ignored me.

"And what about your sister? Did you consider her when you made your plans?"

"I took good care of Shelby. I even made sure she did her homework. Ask her." I had worked out everything perfectly. She just refused to see it.

"That's beside the point. You know better. We've told you a million times you can't go places without letting us know."

"But I did let you know. I left a note." I stomped over to the fridge, pulled the slip of paper from under the magnet, and threw it at her. "See?"

"Not good enough. You don't go without verbal permission. Not after dark. Uh uh."

"Nothing's ever good enough for you. You're always telling me to grow up. Take on more responsibilities." My eyes were stinging.

"That's enough, Elizabeth Jane Ash. You left

without permission and imposed on Mr. Paulsen. You're grounded."

"But Mom —"

"I said, enough already. You think you're grown up? Then take your consequences like a grown-up and keep quiet. Go to your room and reflect on your actions."

It was so unfair, but I went.

I threw myself on the bed and buried my face into a pillow. Hot tears rolled off my cheeks, soaking the sham.

Parents. Who could understand them? They wanted you to act like an adult. But only when it suited them. At least that's what mine were like.

Can't get home in time to be there for the kids after school? Well, Lizzie's reliable enough to have a key. The girls will only be alone for half an hour. Meeting's running late? Lizzie's capable enough to scramble eggs in the microwave. Right? Want a night out on the town? Lizzie's responsible enough to babysit Shelby. After all, it's only for a couple of hours. But let Lizzie act like an adult, figure out a problem all by herself, cover all the bases, and have it work perfectly? Well. We can't have that, can we? She's just a kid. Best put her in her place. Such hypocrites they were.

After my silent rant I felt much better. I wiped my face dry and turned over my pillow to hide the fact that I'd cried like a baby. I thought about putting on my PJs, crawling into bed, and reading, but I was sticky.

"Mom. Can I come out now? I need a bath." I figured after all the years of chasing me to have a shower she'd be pleased as punch.

"You deserve to stay in there all evening. But okay," she answered.

I poured bath salts into the tub. For some reason I needed to feel pretty. I looked at myself in the mirror — mousy brown and average. Some things don't change, but I was growing up, that was quite clear. Still, my parents treated me like a baby. It was so confusing.

Lowering myself into the tub, I inhaled deeply of the moist, perfumed air as the warm water surrounded me. I was going to have a nice long soak.

5 SPICE OF LIFE

"What do you mean you're not going? It was your idea in the first place!" Pam said on Monday.

She was right, I *had* talked her into joining the choir. I had decided to do as many school extracurriculars as I could. It was the only way I'd get variety into my life. My parents only let us sign up for one community club activity. Life's too fast-paced, they complained.

"Look, Pam. It's not as if I don't want to go. But I'm grounded. I can go to school — and that's it." I grabbed a text book and stuffed it into my backpack.

"But this is school, isn't it? I mean it's not, like, going to the mall or my place. Did she say you couldn't go?"

"Well … no. But she didn't say I couldn't go to soccer, either. And that's why I'm in this mess."

"Okay. Phone your mom and ask her if you can stay. Tell her you made this commitment to the group. Parents are big on commitment. Come on." Her small hand grabbed my wrist and started pulling.

Man, sometimes Pam is brilliant. Mom actually said I could stay if I kept Shelby with me. Now tell me how this was any different than at soccer that night?

I didn't point it out to my mom, though. I wasn't that stupid, but it sure made me feel superior. I walked into Language Arts with this big grin on my face. I was having an imaginary conversation with my mother — pointing out how two-faced she was. I was so involved in my daydream when I lowered my butt into the seat behind Pam that I never noticed someone was sitting there until it was too late. Everyone started laughing. Thank goodness the teacher hadn't been in the room.

"Every time I turn around you're climbing into my lap."

Oh man. Of all the people, why'd it have to be the Brock-o-li? My face flushed red. I fled straight to the girls' washroom.

I rested my forehead on the cool cement wall. Before I knew it, tears streamed down my face. This is crazy, I thought. I don't know why I'm crying. It's not that big a deal. Just an embarrassing moment.

When the door to the washroom squeaked open, I quickly dried my tears on my sleeve. I turned to the sink closest to me, twisted on the cold water tap, and splashed my face.

"Lizzie, you'd better hurry up. Mrs. McGaughy was wondering why you weren't in class, so I told her you had PMS, 'kay?"

No, it wasn't okay.

"Jeez, Pam! Boy can you ever be dumb sometimes. Did you have to tell the whole class that?"

"Silly. I didn't, like, say it out loud. I just whispered it to the teacher, 'kay?"

"Okay. But — it's not PMS."

"Yeah, well, it could be. You've been, like, moody lately. And we're twelve, so there's that hormone thing happening. Y'know — remember family life class?"

"You're nuts. I just felt stupid — that's all. You've been just as moody. And both of us know that it's got nothing to do with PMS, don't we? Just B-O-Y. So knock it off."

I slipped into a seat at the back of the class and acted as if nothing had happened. Nobody seemed to notice. They were quietly doing their work.

★ ★ ★

The next day in Foods we made soup. Alex and Rosa, the other two girls in our kitchen, chopped the veggies while Pam and I prepared the rest of the ingredients.

"Two tablespoons of butter ... half a teaspoon of garlic powder," I called.

"Oh, Lizzie can't we, like, leave out the garlic? I don't know if I like it," Pam pleaded.

"No. We have to put it in. The soup won't taste right if we don't." There was no way I was going to let Pam change the recipe. I loved garlic — garlic toast, shrimp in black bean and garlic sauce, honey garlic chicken — my mouth watered just thinking about them.

"Then can't we put less?"

"Trust me, you can never have too much garlic. It will taste great. You'll see."

She wrinkled her little nose as she poured the powder into the spoon.

"Phee-ew. We're not putting that stuff in. I hate it." Alex added the carrots she had cut to the broth.

"You don't like it, Alex? We'll leave it out." Rosa poured the garlic powder back into the bottle.

Even the Italian voted against me, I grumbled to myself.

"Got any garlic powder?" Brock asked over the adjoining counter.

"Yeah. Lots. They won't let me put any in the soup," I complained.

"She, like, thinks you can't have too much of the stuff." Pam handed our bottle to him.

I turned my back to the others and concentrated on stirring the soup. They were laughing at something the Brock-o-li had said. I ignored them and began dishing out the finished product.

"Hey, Lizzie?" It was James from Brock's kitchen. He was one of the new kids, kind of quiet and mousy looking — like me. I didn't know him at all. "Why don't you have some of our soup? Pam said you liked garlic and *we* put it in."

"Really? Thanks. That's nice of you." I took the bowl that he handed me.

Pam was passing bowls across the counter, too. "Here, try ours."

"Well, how is it?" James looked at me expectantly. "Too much salt? Pepper? I don't like spicy foods myself."

I took a spoonful. The garlic flavour was pretty strong.

"Just perfect," I lied. There was no way I was going to admit that there was too much of my favourite flavour. "I'd have some more, if there was any."

I was surprised when he handed me a second bowl. The teacher's so cheap that there's usually just enough for one small serving each. I forced myself to down it.

As we cleaned up, I noticed that there was a lot of whispering and giggling in the other kitchens. "What do you think's going on?" I handed Pam the dish I had just washed.

"What do you mean?" She shook her head.

Rosa and Alex laughed.

"There. Look. Didn't you see that?" Angie, who played defence on our soccer team, was pointing at us.

"Oh, Lizzie. They're probably talking about ... Alex's ... new hair."

"New hair? It's only a glorified ponytail for heaven's sake."

"Yeah, well, you know." Alex pulled herself up to

her full height. "Some kids can be pretty nasty to you when you're good-looking."

Conceited, I thought.

The ride back from Foods was weird. All the kids sat together in the rear of the bus. Usually we sat in small groups scattered through the vehicle.

"That was great soup, wasn't it?" said Angie, blowing a lock of her rusty hair off her forehead.

There was a general murmur of agreement.

"How about you, Lizzie? Did you like the boys' stuff?" Pam asked.

"Yeah, it was fine."

The kids around us started to snigger.

"All right. What gives?" I grabbed Pam's arm and shook it.

"What? What?" She gave me this innocent look.

The sniggering turned to guffaws.

I leaned forward and brought my face close to hers — my brown eyes boring into her. "Tell — me — now."

Pam recoiled. She reached into her pocket, pulled out some gum and offered it to me.

"I said *now*, Pam. And I don't want your gum."

"Oh, Lizzie. Like, you really do. They're for bad breath, 'kay? Brock put half a bottle of garlic powder in their soup."

The kids rolled with laughter.

"He did what? Did you know before I ate it? If you did, I'm going to kill you." I glared at her.

"Please don't be mad, Lizzie, 'kay? It's your own fault. You kept saying you could never have too much garlic and ... "

I got up and moved to the front of the bus.

"*Lizzie*. It was just a joke." Pam called after me.

Some joke. I covered my face with my hands, exhaled through my mouth, and inhaled through my nose to check my breath. It reeked of garlic. I decided to stay on the bus and go home for lunch, to brush my teeth and use some mouthwash.

"Aren't you coming, Lizzie?" Pam asked as she got off the bus.

I didn't answer her. No way was I letting her off the hook that easy.

When I got home, I made myself a tomato sandwich. As I put the veggies back into the crisper, I saw the parsley. I grabbed the bag and stuffed the curly leaves into my sandwich. Mom had once told me parsley was good for your breath. I prayed it would work.

Before leaving for school, I brushed my teeth. I ran the bristles over my tongue and gums as well. Then I gargled with mouthwash until it stung. I tested my breath — minty, with only a hint of garlic.

When the buzzer rang, I waited outside as long as I could before going in. I hoped Pam had gone to band already. She had. I grabbed my clarinet from the locker and took my seat.

"What's that awful smell?" The Brock-o-li sniffed the air.

The others sniffed also.

"Phew."

"Gross."

"It smells like a dragon's breath. Lizard's breath. Or is it *Lizzie's* breath?" Brock was in fine form.

Angry tears formed in the corners of my eyes. I bit down hard on the inside of my cheek to keep them from falling. Placing my clarinet to my lips, I played the scales, waiting for the teacher to come, waiting for the day to end.

6 TOO MUCH GARLIC?

"Excuse me, pumpkin."

I moved my chair slightly so Dad could get into the refrigerator.

"Something's gone bad in there. You can smell it." He grabbed the milk, sniffed it, then drizzled some into his morning coffee.

Mom squeezed passed him, sniffed and closed the door. "Eww. Something does reek. I can't imagine what it could be, the kids cleaned it just the other day. Please check it after school, girls. Hurry up, if you want a ride with me."

I grabbed my runners and sat on the stairs to put them on. Dad patted my head as he passed by. He took two steps towards the door, came back, and inhaled.

"Ally, come here. That smell — I think I've found out what it is."

Both Mom and Shelby came. A lot of sniffing took place.

"Mom, it's Lizzie. She smells like my fingers do

when I peel garlic for you." Shelby's green eyes were round like saucers.

"I do not." I couldn't believe she would tell such lies.

"She's right, Lizzie. That strong odour really is coming from you," Dad said quietly.

"Oh, Lizzie. Late or not, go up and shower." My mother shook her head.

"I had a shower this morning. And a bath last night." I stamped my foot.

"Well, then just go up and change those smelly clothes." Dad tried to smooth things over.

"I did. I changed everything."

"Even your undies?" asked Shelby.

"Yes, even my undies. As if it's any of your business." I stuck my tongue out at her.

"Something's definitely wrong. You do smell of garlic. Are you feeling sick?" Mom was all concerned, so she felt my forehead.

"I'm fine," I wailed. "At least I think so. It must have been the soup. In Foods yesterday I ate two big bowls of it. I didn't know that Brock had put half a bottle of garlic powder in the pot. You can't die from too much garlic, can you?"

"I highly doubt it. But ... but ... you won't have to worry about vampires." Dad burst out laughing.

"Aaron, stop it. The poor kid's upset for heaven's sake ... " Mom tried to hold back her giggles but lost it too.

Shelby looked at our parents, hesitated for a moment, then joined them.

I started to cry.

Mom got control of herself. "Oh, sweetie, I'm sorry." She put her arm around me and squeezed me tight. "I've never heard of this kind of thing happening."

"My health teacher told us of a lady who fed her baby so many carrots that the baby's skin turned orange. I think it must have been just a tinge of colour. Not bright like a pumpkin. This could be the same kind of thing, right?" Shelby added her two bits. Trust smarty-pants to know something about everything.

"Maybe," said Mom.

"But — why don't I smell it? I — can't — smell — anything," I said between my sobs.

"I guess the same reason people with B.O. don't know they have it. Our brains must block out stinky smells that are always around. I bet I'm right." My sister grinned from ear to ear.

"I bet you are, munchkin." Dad tousled her curls.

"What can I do, Mom?" I swiped at my tears.

"Beats me, I haven't a clue. Maybe we should call Dr. Armstrong." She reached for the hall phone.

"No. Please, Mom, just let me stay home. I can't go to school smelling like this. I'll catch up on the work, I promise." I wiped my tears on the sleeve of my sweatshirt.

"I suppose ... all right. Missing one day won't hurt

you." She looked at her watch. "I'll call the school from work. I'm going to be late as it is."

"Can I stay home, too?" Shelby asked.

"No. Now get moving."

"Don't tell anyone," I yelled at their backs.

At first, I walked aimlessly around the house trying to figure out what to do. Then I decided to look up garlic on the Internet. I scrolled through reams of tips on how to use it. There were enough recipes to keep even me happy cooking until I was eighty. One of the sites had all kinds of data on the chemicals in garlic. *Boring.* I forced myself to read it. Diallyl disulfide — that's what was making me reek. It could give you bad breath just by handling loads of garlic. And, yes, parsley fought the odour.

I stumbled onto a site about garlic warding off vampires. The stuff was so cool that I forgot why I started the Web search. I went from vampires to werewolves to the Loch Ness monster. The day just flew by. By the time Shelby came home from school, I figured I was an expert on all things weird and wonderful.

"You still stink," she said as she read over my shoulder.

"Thanks. Just what I needed to hear," I mumbled. I had actually enjoyed my time alone. Shelby had brought me crashing down to reality.

"Sorry, Lizzie. I didn't mean to be nasty, really I didn't." She sniffed hard a couple of times. "I don't think it's as bad as this morning."

"I'm going to take a bath." I stomped out of the room.

I shampooed my hair three times. Sticking the plug in the drain, I turned on the taps full blast. I poured half a bottle of bubble bath into the swirling water. If that didn't make me smell good, nothing would. The tub filled with foam, just like in the movies.

I soaked until my skin wrinkled and the water turned cold. I was wiping myself dry when Dad came home.

"Where is my malodorous vampire slayer?" he called. "The house is filled with the scent of flowers. I don't think I can find her on my own."

"Ha ha. You're so funny I forgot to laugh," I yelled through the bathroom door.

★ ★ ★

"Do I still stink?" I asked the next morning.

Shelby sniffed. "No ... well, maybe a little. I don't know ... "

I decided not to take any chances. I shampooed and showered again — rubbing myself raw. Then for an added bonus, I sprayed on Mom's perfume.

"Whoa. Yesterday the herb patch — today the English Garden." Dad made like he was falling out of the kitchen chair and ended up spilling coffee all over the table. Shelby laughed.

"Aaron." My mother glared at him. Then she turned and smiled at me. Gently she ran her fingers through my brown locks. "You look lovely today, sweetie. That shade of red complements your complexion."

She was pretending yesterday never happened and I loved her for it.

"Thanks, Mom." I kissed her cheek.

Grabbing my lunch from the fridge, I headed for the door.

"Mr. Henchel has early tutorials today. I think I'll go and find out what I missed. Bye," I called over my shoulder.

"Wait. Take your coat. There's a chill in the air. Here's a muffin to eat on the way."

"Oh, *Mom*." I could tell she wasn't going to cave, so I grabbed my soccer jacket, pocketed the muffin and ran to Paddington.

"Hey, Lizard-breath, where were you yesterday?"

Just my luck — Brock. He was sitting on the floor in the school's front hall.

"I was home. Sick, if you must know."

"Garlic overdose, Lizard-breath?"

"None of your business," I snapped. It irked me more because he was right.

"I'm hurt, Lizard-breath."

"Look who's calling who a lizard?" The crack about breath was getting on my nerves. I noticed the old-man hat sitting on top of his backpack. "That coat and hat you wear are so outdated you're a dinosaur."

"Why, thank you, Lizard-breath. T-rex was the king of his domain."

"Don't flatter yourself. I was thinking of the brontosaurus and his pea brain. After all, you're here for math help, right?"

"Wrong-o, volleyball practice. Sorry to disappoint you, Lizard-breath."

"Knock it off."

"Whatever you say, Lizard-breath."

"Gaah!" I fled to the math room when Mr. Henchel unlocked the door to the junior-high wing.

By the time the morning buzzer went, I was all caught up. As I walked into the hall, I bumped into Pam.

"Oh, Lizzie, you're back," she squealed and hugged me.

Her good spirits rubbed off on me. I was feeling like my old self when I went into Language Arts.

"Look, everybody, Lizard-breath is back. She got over her garlic overdose." The jerk was at it again.

"Cut the crap you ... you ... brock-e-osaurus brain." I had meant to say brachiosaurus but somehow it came out wrong.

"You mean they've discovered a super-smart dinosaur? All right!" Brock raised his fist triumphantly.

"Oooh! That's *so* cute. Brock-e-osaurus. I have this

little plush dinosaur I've had, like, forever. I think I'll rename him that." Pam dripped honey.

"Oh man." What a waste of a good insult. She had taken my words and made them sound mushy. "I don't want to hear you use that name around me. Got it?" I plunked myself into the first desk by the door.

"Okay." Pam glanced wistfully at Brock before sliding into the seat beside me.

★ ★ ★

That evening we had a serious soccer practice. Vern said we needed to get into better condition, so we'd been running laps to begin each session. This time we also worked on our starts and stops by sprinting across the gym playing Red Light, Green Light. Even though we had to work hard, our coach still made the practices fun.

The thing about indoor soccer is that it's a totally different game than the outdoor one. Sure, you kick the ball and head it, and a lot of the rules are the same — like only the goalie can touch the ball with her hands. But the feel is different. It's fast-paced like hockey or ringette. There are only five players per side if you don't count the goalie, and you sub in on the fly. In seconds, the whole game can change. On a hard two-minute shift you get exhausted. Thank goodness the pitch is fairly short because you'd die if it wasn't. It looks like a rink with carpet instead of ice. You're surrounded by boards so that low kicks don't go out of bounds. You can ricochet the ball off the walls — a great player learns to play the angles.

I wasn't quite there yet, but Vern had said if I kept on trying I would be. That practice I focused on working the wall and by the time the hour-and-a-half was over, I felt I was finally getting the hang of things.

My heart soared when Coach said, "Nice work, Lizzie."

7 TROUBLE WITH TACOS

"My, my. Your last Foods lab. How time flies," Ms. Oliver said, rubbing her hands together. "Well, let's get started. We'll be making tacos. Send someone to the front to pick up your kitchen's ingredients, please. You will notice the packets of lime drink. Take one. My treat."

My eyes teared as I chopped the onions. I tossed them into the hot frying pan — sautéed onions, yummy.

"We're leaving out the garlic." Alex was obviously telling, not asking, me.

I kept my mouth shut, just nodded. Since the soup lab, I was no longer allowed to measure spices. *They* didn't trust *me*. Go figure.

I fixed my taco the way I liked it, with lots of tomato and green pepper, light on the lettuce.

"Do me a favour?" Rosa asked as she handed me a glass of limeade. With the back of her hand she pushed her dark locks off her face. "Fix me a taco, please. I have to wipe up this sticky mess. I spilled sugar all over."

"Sure. Let me put this down first. Okay?" I set my

food on the table and grabbed another plate. "How do you like it?"

"Loaded." She swiped at the counter with a drippy dishcloth.

I spooned a generous amount of grated cheddar on top of Rosa's taco. By the time I was finished, she was sitting down with Alex and Pam at our table.

My mouth was watering. I loved tacos. I took a big bite of mine. Fire. My mouth was on fire! I grabbed my drink. It tasted foul. *Gag. Cough, cough.* But I needed to put out the fire, so I took another swig. Garlic. I ran to the sink and spewed out the liquid, gagging and coughing.

"What did you guys do to my food?" I whispered hoarsely, trying to catch my breath.

"Nothing." Rosa's dark eyes opened as big as saucers.

The three of them looked as stunned as I was.

"Brock," Pam said quietly. "He came to borrow some salt."

I looked down at my plate. How could I have missed that it wasn't from our set? Suddenly I became aware of the laughter in the next kitchen and my blood boiled. I picked up the glass and plate and walked up to Brock. I mushed the plateful into his face, poured the drink over his head, and then I slapped him.

There was a communal gasp. Ms. Oliver stood frozen in shock. Here and there giggling broke out and it lifted the teacher's spell.

"Lizzie Ash. This is too much. Clean up that mess. Then go see the principal."

"But... but it's not my fault. He put garlic in my drink and switched my taco with one laced with chilis." I pointed at Brock, who was at the sink washing the food from his face.

"I don't care what he did. Your behaviour is inexcusable."

"Ms. Oliver, Lizzie's right. I did spoil her food. Please don't be so hard on her." He blinked his red eyes rapidly.

"Your behaviour's been nothing to brag about from day one, either. So, if you feel you're partially to blame, you can help her clean up and join her in Mr. Millan's office."

★ ★ ★

"Elizabeth Ash. Brock Maguire. You can go in now."

Reality hit me in the face. I had never been sent to the office before. Wiping my sweaty palms on my t-shirt, I stood up and waited for Brock to go ahead of me.

"Sit down." Mr. Millan waved at some chairs across from his desk. "Now, what's this all about?"

I handed him Ms. Oliver's note. He placed it unread on his desk.

"First, I want your version." He gazed from me to Brock — and then back again.

I tried to speak but my mouth went dry. I swallowed hard and tried again.

"I ... I threw food on him and slapped him in the face, sir," I managed to squeak out.

"But it's my fault. I switched Lizzie's taco and limeade with stuff I had spiked with chili flakes and garlic. I don't blame her for being mad."

"That may be so, but reacting with violence or being disrespectful is not to be taken lightly."

"No, sir." Brock and I answered in unison.

Mr. Millan picked up and read Ms. Oliver's note. "I gather this is your last class of this session. Bad timing. I'd hate to have to drag Paddington's principal into this. Tell you what — for your punishment, I'd like you two to come back after school one day soon. To help Ms. Oliver."

"Sir, I ... I ... I can't. I have to babysit my younger sister after school," I stammered.

"Me too," said the Brock-o-li.

Copycat, I was sure he was lying.

"One moment." Mr. Millan opened his door and called to his secretary. "Mrs. R, could you call Paddington School to check if they have an in-service day in the near future? For the junior high only. One that doesn't coincide with one of ours, please."

He let us sit silently, stewing in our own juices. The secretary poked her head around the corner once more. "There's an afternoon in-service two weeks from

Friday. The good news is that on Friday afternoons, Ms. Oliver has a Paddington grade eight class. Since they won't be coming, she'll be free."

"Good work. Thanks. All right, we'll see you two back here on ... " He glanced on the calendar. "Ah ... the sixth of November. Now, go apologize to your teacher and fellow students for disrupting their class."

The story of what I did to Brock spread through the school like wildfire, but nobody bothered to explain why I did it. So, all week long, I was known as Lizzie Limeade the Taco-tosser. Each day I hoped that someone would do something to provide another topic of conversation — no such luck.

I was so glad when Friday came. Maybe the kids would find better things to occupy their minds with over the weekend. I knew I would, because the indoor soccer season was starting. Our first game was scheduled for Saturday at nine-forty-five in the morning. Shelby's was on Sunday.

That night I set out my uniform, shin pads, and runners. I had tried to talk Mom into buying special indoor soccer shoes.

"An unnecessary expense. Regular runners work just fine. Mr. Hiebert said so," she insisted and she wouldn't budge.

I went to bed early. What a joke. I was too excited so I tossed and turned, barely sleeping at all. Morning couldn't come fast enough. I crawled out of bed in the dark. I had showered, eaten a bowl of puffed wheat, and brushed my teeth before anyone else woke up. Even then, it was only Shelby.

We snuggled under the throw in the family room watching early-morning cartoons.

"My, my. What a Kodak moment." Dad padded through the room, yawning and stretching, on his way to grab a cup of coffee. He said he didn't function too well without it. I never noticed any difference. He just wasn't a crabby person.

"So, what time is that game of yours?" he asked.

"Nine-forty-five. But we have to be there a half-hour early."

"Hmm ... eight-ten. Better go up and make myself human." He rubbed his stubbly chin. "Don't want people thinking Bigfoot watches soccer."

I followed him up to change into my stuff. I admired myself in the mirror. Today I felt better than average. The power that seemed to be in the uniform on the first day was still there. I was sure we would win the game.

Last year my parents had worked out that Dad would be my chauffeur and Mom would be Shelby's. I wished that they would both come to my games sometimes. But at least they didn't just drop us off, like some of the other parents. They stayed and cheered us on.

By the time we got to Court Sports, most of the girls were already there — huddled with our fans in a corner by the front doors. There was no place else to go because the game before ours was still on and their spectators filled the bleachers.

"Oh shoot. I forgot there's no point in coming early. Next game, ladies — fifteen minutes before game time is plenty. Follow me." Vern herded us toward the bleachers. "We're home today."

There are only a few indoor soccer pitches in Winnipeg, so most teams practise in gyms and take turns being home or away at the games.

We excused our way to the corner of the large cement building that doubled as the home team change room. A plywood partition separated it from the rest of the space.

None of us actually changed there. We had our uniforms on under our clothes.

I stripped off my tearaway pants, tossed them on top of my jacket, and started to stretch.

"Okay, ladies. Gather round. Let's fill out the game sheet. I want to make sure your names and numbers are correct," Vern bellowed over the noise.

Once we were all accounted for, he gave his pep talk.

"For the last few weeks we've worked hard. Now it's time to show what you can do. Remember what we practised. Look for the open man. Call for the pass. Go to the ball, don't wait for it to come to you. And use the wall. If you get tired, put up your hand.

We'll get you off as soon as we can. You ladies have a lot of spunk. Channel that energy and you'll do all right."

Sometime during the pep talk, the other game had ended and the corner filled with kids in orange uniforms trying to retrieve their belongings.

"All right, let's give them some room. Get out there and warm up." He grabbed the equipment and headed for our bench.

The coach tossed balls out of the bag, while we ran a warm-up lap.

"Okay, pick a partner and practise passing," Vern called. "Jen, you're in goal. Put on the shirt and gloves. Alex, I want you to warm her up."

Pam and I paired off with each other and kicked the ball back and forth. When the ref blew the whistle, Vern called us to the bench and listed the starting lineup.

Yes! I was on at left forward.

As we lined up for the kickoff I rubbed my fingers across the glossy lettering of my shirt. There was power there all right — the tips of my digits tingled.

The ball bounced my way. I captured it with my body and took off up the side of the pitch. The Laser centre challenged me. I faked a pass and went around her, deking another player. I shot. In it went.

I was stunned. The first goal of the game — first goal of our season, in the first minutes of play, from me? It had to be the uniform.

I beamed as the Pythons high-fived and patted my back.

Another faceoff. Alex stole the ball and passed it up my side. It arced towards me, dropping a few strides short. Crap. It bounced in typical indoor-soccer fashion — erratically. When ball meets rug, it seems to have a mind of its own. A red shirt got it and dribbled it along the wall. I blocked her, kicking at the ball as she tried to advance. For a minute we struggled, getting nowhere. Then I won. The ball popped out behind her and Angie picked it up. She passed it to Rosa, who one-timed it straight at the goalie. Nuts, the kid stopped it. No problem. She gave it a long boot right at me. I headed it. No kidding. I didn't even think about getting hurt. I just did it.

Alex picked it up and dribbled. She shot wide and the play went down the other side towards our goal. Jen saved a weak shot, then threw the ball to Angie, our right defence. She captured the ball with her chest, then dribbled upfield. The next thing I knew the play was coming up my side again. I forced the action along the wall, because that's the stuff I love. Struggling along the boards. Just kicking — and kicking — till the ball pops loose. I forced the red shirt to slowly inch back to the midline before the ball rolled free. Rosa picked it up and was gone.

I stood holding the wall for a second, puffing. Then, I raised my hand to be subbed off.

"Great shift, Lizzie." Vern patted my head as I squeezed past him on the bench.

"What's gotten into you? You were awesome," Pam called as she jumped onto the pitch to sub off Rosa.

I shrugged in answer. Dumb luck. Things went my way, that's all.

By the end of the game, I wasn't so sure everything had just gone my way. It had to be magic — the power in the new uniform. I hadn't ducked from the ball, or hesitated; I had played the game of my life. I hadn't scored again, but then no one else had either. I'd just felt invincible. We'd won on my miraculous goal.

"Do you believe in magic?" I asked Dad on the drive home.

"Depends what you mean. Love is magical. Seeing you kids being born was pure magic. Ask your Mom —"

"*Dad.* You know I don't mean that." So I told him about the tingling fingers and how I'd felt powerful out on the pitch.

"Honey, I think you played well because you felt confident, not because of magic."

"But what about the tingling fingers?"

"Static. When you rubbed your shirt you caused static electricity. Right, Dad?" Shelby said from the back seat.

"No doubt, sweetie." He reached over and fingered my sleeve. "This is a synthetic fabric, Lizzie."

Smarty-pants, I thought. Trust her to come up with a logical reason. I looked down at my shirt. Suddenly, it just felt ordinary.

8 HUMBLE PIE

"Hey Lizzie —"

I jumped, even though the words were whispered. The stuff I was carrying flew into the air and scattered among the milling students. I watched in dismay as my science text was kicked into a grade nine classroom.

"Now look what you've done. You stupid moron." I struggled to retrieve my things from amid the feet.

"Sorry. Here, let me help." Brock bent down beside me. "So, who was that chicky I saw you with on Sunday?"

"You must have been seeing things. On Sunday I was doing homework." I swept some crumpled papers back into my binder.

"Nuh uh. You were there. At the indoor soccer game." He grabbed a pen in danger of being trampled.

"Saturday. I played on Saturday. Blockhead." I snatched the pen from his hand.

"It was Sunday and you weren't playing. You were sitting in the stands."

"Oh yeah..." I remembered Shelby's game.

"I see the light's finally come on, eh, Dizzy-Lizzie?" he called from the open door as he rescued my text-book. "So? Who was she?"

"I wasn't with any 'chicky.' Must have been some-one who just happened to sit beside me."

"Come on, Dizzy — think." He handed me my book. "You were talking to her a lot. You know, the hottie with the blond hair down to here." He placed his hand at shoulder level. "The one in the red suit."

"Red suit...? Mom?" My eyes got big and round.

"That was your mother? She didn't look like a mother."

"What the heck do you mean by that?" I glared at him.

His face reddened. "You know, all the other moth-ers wear jeans, track suits — that kind of thing. They don't come all dressed up to a soccer game."

I placed my fists on my hips and stuck out my chin. "What of it?" I said.

"Nothing. I just thought she was a model or some-thing. Is she?"

"No. She's a designer. She had a meeting that af-ternoon. That's why she was all dressed up," I lied. I don't know why I felt the need to explain my mom's outfit. Mom always dressed beautifully, and normally I was proud of how she looked.

As we dropped into adjacent seats in French class,

I changed the subject. "What were you doing there?"

"What do you think? I went to watch my sister, Ashley, play. Duh." He turned sideways in his seat and stretched his legs into the aisle. "That team's something else."

"No kidding. They owned the other team. Eleven to nothing!"

"So, who were you watching?"

"My sister, Shelby," I said proudly. I loved seeing her play soccer. She dodged around the larger players and squeezed through holes that looked impossible. She fought like a badger along the boards. On Sunday she was awesome.

"Oh, was she the tiny blond girl that kicked butt?" Brock asked. "Cute. Except for being so small, she's your mother's daughter."

And I'm not, I thought. That's what he really means, right? It's not my fault I take after my father. I wanted the floor to open and swallow me up. I turned away from him and faced the front.

"Hey, guys. Did you get your tickets for the dance on Friday? I heard they were only going to sell them till, like, noon today, so I rushed and bought mine. It's *so* unfair to stop selling tickets on Wednesday when the dance isn't — "

"Pam, slow down. You've been moving so fast you're way ahead of yourself. It's only Monday." Brock laughed.

"Oh." She tossed her head. "Well it's an easy mistake. Wednesday's timetable starts out the same as Monday's, y'know."

I shook my head. "Whatever." Sometimes Pam is so Pam, you just accept her for who she is.

She was standing beside my desk as if she were waiting for something.

"What?" I asked.

She whispered through clenched teeth. "*Lizzie. Our deal. Remember? Me between you and you-know-who?*" She tossed her head in Brock's direction.

"Oh. Right."

Brock raised his eyebrows when I picked up my books and moved over one desk.

"Are we playing musical chairs?" he asked.

"Not we, just me," I answered.

★ ★ ★

"So what're you going to wear?" Pam asked as we were changing for Gym.

"What kind of stupid question is that? My gym clothes. Duh." I answered

Pam laughed. "No, silly, I mean to the Halloween dance."

"I'm not going."

"But Lizzie, you just have to go. I need you for, y'know, moral support. This is my chance to dance with

Brock. I know I'll have to make the first move. He hasn't even hinted that he wants to go out with me. Do you think he's just too shy?"

Oh brother, she was doing the doe-eye thing again. I sighed. "Okay. I'll buy my ticket tomorrow."

"Oh, Lizzie! You won't be sorry. So, like, what are you going to wear? Want to go as a two-headed monster?"

"Heck no," I answered in horror. "Then I'd have to dance with Brock when you did."

"Oh yeah." Pam giggled. "And I want him all to myself."

"I'm not going to dress up at all."

"You get half your money back if you do," Pam insisted.

After supper she dragged me to the thrift shop on Meadowood.

"I want to look glamorous. Kind of like your mother. My mom says I'm sure to find something suitable here."

Pam went through a rack of ladies' evening clothes and picked out a purple monstrosity. "What do you think?"

While I struggled to find the right words, she burst out laughing. "Got ya. It's too *Cruella De Vil*, don't you think? I'm going for the sophisticated look." She rifled through the rack again.

I'd never been in a thrift store before, so I sort of

wandered off, browsing. There was all kinds of junk but there was some great stuff that looked brand new, too. You could dress real smart on the cheap, if you knew your labels. That explained Brock's cool clothes.

I was exploring through some really neat leather jackets when I looked up, and there it was. Staring me in the face was a coat identical to the one the Brock-o-li wore. An idea started to form in my brain. I put the coat on and frantically looked for the matching accessory — the old-man hat. There — a shelf full, along the wall. I grabbed one and put it on. It dropped down, covering my eyes. I put it back and rummaged until I found a smaller one, then I went to find Pam.

"Well? What do you think?" I twirled in front of her.

"Neat-o. We can, like, go as a couple. But you'll need a suit, too, okay?"

It wasn't quite the reaction I was hoping for.

She dragged me to where the men's dress clothing was. Thank goodness, nothing there looked right to Pam.

"Maybe you can wear something of your dad's," she said.

"Maybe," I lied. "Have you found anything yet?"

She nodded. "I've narrowed it down to two. Help me decide, okay?"

She held up the dresses. One was a low-cut, beaded thing in red satin. The other was a simple black knit with silver threads running through the slinky fabric.

"The black one," I said.

"Really?" Pam sounded disappointed.

I could have said "if you wear that red thing, the neckline is going to hang to your belly button," but I didn't.

"It's got to be the black one because it's easy enough to alter. Mom says knits are great to work with and look — you'd lose the best part, the beadwork, if you shortened the red dress. That would be a shame, wouldn't it?"

"Yeah, I guess you're right." She stared wistfully at the red satin for a moment, then quickly put it back. "Let's get out of here, okay? Before I, like, change my mind."

I clutched my purchase tightly as we climbed onto the bus. Giggling internally, I wondered what the Brock-o-li would say when I turned up at the dance. It was the best seven dollars I'd ever spent. Then I got to thinking — why would a kid, even if he was poor, buy this geeky outfit? For a few dollars more, he could have had one of those cool leather jackets or a team sports jacket.

I couldn't wait till the dance.

That Friday evening I pulled on my jeans and a black t-shirt, the uniform of every twelve-year-old boy I know. I tucked my long hair into a curly orange clown wig and jammed on the hat. Then I put on the coat and admired myself in the mirror before skipping down the stairs.

"Curly, from the Three Stooges. Right?" my Dad guessed.

"Oh, no, Daddy. I think she's trying to look like Brock Ma—" She stopped speaking because I was glaring at her.

"How did you guess, Dad?" Quickly, I slipped out the door to wait for Pam. I figured it was safer on the front stairs.

"Oh, couldn't you find a suit? You don't look right to be my date. And what's with that dorky wig?" Pam said as she strutted up the sidewalk in her elegant black dress.

She didn't get it even though Shelby had. Smart Shelby. I decided not to tell her in case it ticked her off. It would be my private joke.

"I'm Curly, from the Three Stooges," I said. Whoever they are, I thought.

She stared at me for a moment. "The coat and hat are okay, but that wig — it's more like Harpo's from the Marx Brothers, except he's blond. At least I think he is. The movies are in black and white. Whatever. At least it's a costume. Don't I look perfect?" She patted her hair.

"You're soo hot, *hisssss*," I said, scorching my finger on her shoulder, but I was stunned that she knew who Curly was.

The latest hit was blaring through the gym doors when we got to the dance. The DJ had set up in the back of the room across from the front doors. Each grade level had staked out its territory. The grade nines had grabbed the choicest spot — the dimly-lit back corner of the room. Grade eights claimed the area closest to the canteen. That left the space in front of the gym doors for the grade seven kids, right under the noses of the teachers who were taking tickets. The middle of the gym — the dance floor — was empty except for the occasional student crossing to their appropriate area.

As we walked up to the seventh graders, some of the kids started to giggle.

"Hey. They're, like, laughing at you. I guess your Curly costume's okay," Pam said.

"Curly, shmurly." Alex stopped laughing long enough to spit out, "that's Brock Maguire, if you ask me."

Pam stood back and looked at me.

"Oh, right. Get a load of the curly clown wig. She doesn't look at all like him. To think I was giving you credit for knowing the Stooges," she sniffed at Alex. Turning back to me she said, "Anyway... I don't see Brock. Do you?"

I looked closely through the crowd. "Unless he's wearing one heck of a disguise, I don't think he's here. Maybe he isn't coming."

"Oh yes he is. I took care of that. I bribed James to

make sure Brock came. I have his five bucks right here."
She shook her fancy evening bag in my face.

Suddenly she reached over and grabbed my arm.
Her fingers dug into me as the grip tightened and her
smile slowly faded.

"Oh my gosh, oh my gosh. Don't turn around
Lizzie. He's, like, *here*," she whispered.

"Oh, for heaven's sake, Pam, isn't that what you
wanted?"

"Yeah. But what am I going to do? What am I going to say?"

Motormouth at a loss for words? I highly doubt it,
I thought.

"Get a grip. Why are you making such a big deal
out of nothing? Act normal. You have no problem talking to him every day at school. Now let go of my arm,
you're hurting me."

"Oops. Sorry, Lizzie." She took a deep breath. "Okay,
you're right. But it just seems different." She waved and
raised her voice. "Hi Brock, hi James! Over here!"

Crisis over. Motormouth back in gear.

I turned around.

Brock's painted face dropped. Even in the dim light
it looked as if his red-rimmed eyes glistened with mois-
ture. For a moment he worked his crimson mouth as if
trying to say something. Funny, how even a vampire can
look hurt. He swallowed hard, cleared his throat, then
turned up the corners of his lips into a fanged smile.

"Cupcake, I've never seen you look so good. It sure beats how you look normally. Come on, James, let's get a pop." He headed for the canteen.

Pam looked at Brock — then at me — then back at Brock.

"Hey, wait for me, guys! I want a drink too! Let's go, Lizzie." She took off after the boys as fast as her long tight dress would allow.

I didn't follow. Dressing up as Brock wasn't funny anymore. I took off the coat and dropped it along the wall, in the dark and out of my sight.

The DJ put on a hit tune and the dance floor filled. Every teenage girl knew the moves to this one — thanks to videos on MTV that had been played and replayed until the steps were perfected. Angie grabbed my arm and dragged me into the mass of moving bodies.

Thank goodness for being average. My feelings of guilt dulled as I concentrated on the music and getting the moves right.

"Where's your coat?" Pam danced up to me.

"Got too hot," I said.

"Well, you don't look dressed up anymore."

"Did you bring any makeup?" I asked.

"Just some red lipstick and blue eye shadow."

"Good enough. Let's go to the washroom." I headed off the dance floor.

I painted my face to look like a clown. "There. What do you think?"

"Excellent." Pam smiled and my spirits lifted.

I wasn't Brock anymore, so the guilt was gone.

There was a slow dance starting when we came back to the gym. We walked over to where Brock and James were standing.

"Okay, Lizzie, wish me luck," she whispered to me. "I'm going to ask Brock to dance." She leaned towards him. "I haven't danced with you yet, Brock. Come on. Don't you just, like, love this song?"

"Sorry, I don't do slow dances. Some other time, okay?"

"Well, I do. And you haven't danced with me, either." James didn't give Pam a chance to answer. He pulled her into the middle of the crowd, put his arms around her and started to sway to the music.

She was laughing at something he said so I knew she didn't mind. But this left me with Brockula. I sat quietly beside him, trying not to stare, but my eyes kept being drawn to his face. His makeup job was fantastic.

"Hmm, a clown now." He broke the silence. "What a novel idea — to come as a chameleon. Explains why you're always changing on me."

"What can I say? It's in my blood."

"What's that? Did I hear blood?" He leaned towards me, bearing his fangs.

"Don't get any bright ideas, Brockula." I gave him the evil eye.

"Ho ho. A good one. Wouldn't think of it, though.

You eat too much garlic."

I smiled. "Your makeup is awesome. Who did it?"

"What makeup? It's the real thing. I usually wear a mask." He grinned at me.

"I'm serious," I said.

Just then the music changed to a loud, fast song and his answer was lost in the noise. He tried twice to yell above the song but finally gave up.

We lapsed into silence. The music changed to a quieter song and Pam and James kept dancing. Soon the pause in our conversation stretched out too long, becoming unbearable.

"Hey, look over there. They call that supervising," I said, just to say something.

He looked to where I was pointing. Ms. Horton was dancing up a storm with Mr. Nickolic, the principal. They were the most unlikely couple. She, so skinny she could slip under the crack of a closed door. He, so plump that the buttons of his shirt were in danger of popping off and flying into orbit.

"Jack Sprat and his wife — only reversed," Brock said.

"Yeah, yeah. But they're more like Homer and Marge Simpson."

"What about the Simpsons?" Pam asked as she and James returned.

"Oh, nothing. We were just talking about Fred Astaire and Ginger Rogers over there." Brock wagged his chin towards the chaperones, then he and his friend drifted off to the canteen.

I shook my head. Fred Astaire? Ginger Rogers? Where did he get this stuff from?

"You and James seemed to be having a good time," I said.

"Yeah, we did. I thought he was boring, but he's, like, really funny. Come on, let's dance."

And dance we did. With no one in particular, but in the great mass of grade seven kids. We hip-hopped and did the Monster Mash. What a blast! They shut us down at ten-thirty, but by then I was ready to go. My feet were tired and I was sweaty and hot. When the music wasn't on, I couldn't hear clearly because my ears were stuffy. My first school dance and it was all good.

9 FROM THE FRYING PAN INTO THE FIRE

"Lizzie Limeade. Are you coming?"

"Can I come too, Brock?" Pam gave him the doe eyes.

"Whatever turns you on." He scratched his head. "You must be crazy though — to go to detention when you don't have to."

"Exactly! I'm not crazy either. I'll stick with going to the mall, thanks," I said.

"Suit yourself, but Mr. Millan's not going to like it."

"Mr. Millan?"

"The principal of Darwin. It's November the sixth, Lizzie Limeade the Taco Tosser."

"Detention with Ms. Oliver... " It finally dawned on me.

"The light bulb goes on."

Stuffing my book into my backpack, I trudged towards the door.

"Hey, wait up." Pam slammed the locker shut and ran to catch up. "I have to take the same bus to go to the Saint Vital Centre."

I shivered as we waited for the bus. It was the first really cold day of the fall — jacket weather, even for the most diehard sweatshirt wearer. Pam prattled on the whole time. Mostly about the dance and how wonderfully Brock's grandma had done his makeup. Everyone had been blown away by it. Of course, he had won first prize for costume.

Once we were on the bus they started talking about old movies. I stopped paying attention — what did I know about that? I started imagining the yucky job Ms. Oliver might have planned for us. Cleaning the ovens? Bleaching the stains from the white counters?

"Well, Lizzie, what do ya say?" Pam jabbed me in the ribs.

"Huh, what?" I asked.

"I said you two, like, might as well come to the mall and have lunch first. You'll get to Darwin way early."

"Count me out," the Brock-o-li said as he climbed off the bus.

Pam's face fell, but she tried to paste a smile back on.

"I'll treat you, Brock — if you don't have any dough on you," I said. I felt rich because Dad had given me my allowance that morning. Besides, I'd gain brownie points with Pam.

"Mighty big of you, but I don't take charity." He started to walk off.

I grabbed his jacket sleeve and swung him around to face me. "Look, jerk, there's nothing charitable about it. I don't want to face Ms. Oliver alone. Consider it payment for being my bodyguard."

"Well ... if you put it that way." He turned in the direction of the mall and sauntered across the parking lot.

"Ooh, Lizzie, thanks a million." Pam squeezed my arm.

"No problem. Like I said, I have my own motives." We took off after Brock.

"So, what do you want?" I asked him as I dropped my pack on an empty table.

"A taco," he answered innocently.

I glared at him, as if tacos weren't the reason we were here.

"Now what? I feel like a taco. What's wrong with that?"

"Nothing. Go get it yourself." I threw a five-dollar bill at him.

I walked off in the opposite direction to get myself an artery clogger — poutine and a vanilla shake. When I got back, Pam was munching on a taco too, the traitor. Between bites she talked our ears off about Brock's upcoming volleyball tournament.

I slurped the last bit out of my glass. "Let's go face the music."

"Bye, guys. Good luck." Pam waved as she headed for the bookstore.

Brock loaded all our junk onto the tray and dumped it in the garbage.

"Getting into suck-up mode?" I said.

"No. Just cleaning up after myself. Like every decent person should."

My face reddened.

We walked to Darwin in silence. I purposely slowed to let him get ahead of me. I glued my eyes to the green words on his black jacket, *Pythons Boys' Baseball City Champs*.

Jacket? Not the dorky trench coat? Had he bought it from the thrift shop because I had made fun of him at the dance?

I was headed for the shop's entrance when Brock stopped me. "We should go to the office. Make sure that Mr. Millan knows we came."

"I knew that," I lied. "I was going to go there through the school."

"It's shorter this way." He held the front door open for me.

The principal wasn't in but the secretary promised she'd let him know.

"Ms. Oliver, your helpers are here. I'll send them right down to the Foods lab," she said into the intercom.

Our tormentor was waiting for us in the hall.

"Do we have to clean out the ovens?" I was so nervous, I just blurted it out.

"Good heavens, no. You want me to lose my job?" She placed her hand on her forehead. "Trust you two with chemicals? Over my dead body. I have much safer tasks for you troublemakers."

We meekly let her usher us into the room.

"There," she said pointing at a table full of bulk ingredients. "One of you can refill the containers in the lab kitchens while the other takes the steel-wool pads and cleans the stove tops."

"I'll do the stoves. It's safer if Lizard-breath takes care of the spices. There's garlic there. After all, you can handle it better than I can. Right, Lizzie?" He started to chuckle.

I started to steam — first the tacos and now this. Was he ever going to let me live down my mistakes?

"You jerk. I'm sick of you always bringing up the garlic thing. Stop picking on me." I picked up the packet of garlic and was about to launch it at him.

"Oh, dear. Not again." Ms. Oliver had both hands on her face. It looked like she was about to lose it.

"Don't worry, ma'am, there won't be any trouble." He turned to me and shook his head. "Lighten up, Lizzie. All I meant was garlic was dangerous for me. After all, I'm Brockula. I thought you had a sense of humour and could laugh at yourself. Guess I was wrong. That garlic thing is old news — get over it." He snatched up the soap pads and headed to the kitchen farthest from me.

For a moment I stood there blushing with embarrassment, then I got to work.

I finished before Brock, so Ms. Oliver had me straighten shelves. When I was done, he was gone. I trudged to the bus stop hoping he'd be there. I was going to apologize, really I was, but he wasn't there.

It started to snow while I waited for the bus. By the time I got to my stop it was coming down hard — big, wet, blobby flakes. Of course my key gave me some trouble, so I got cold and wet. When the door finally opened, my mood was as stormy as the day. The phone was ringing. I ran to grab it before the caller could hang up.

"Where have you been, Lizzie?" Before I could answer, Mom continued, "Dad and I are going to be late. Meetings again. Please feed Shelby. Her coach will be picking her up at six for soccer practice. Tell her we'll pick her up when it's over. So, where were you? I've been trying to get you all afternoon. I thought you had an in-service."

"Don't you remember anything?" I took my black mood out on her. "You forgot I had detention at Darwin and gave me permission to go to the Saint Vital Centre with Pam. If Brock hadn't remembered, I'd have been in big trouble. I told you about it. You should have remembered."

"It's hard enough keeping track of my own commitments, that's why I write things on the calendar. You should check it every morning. It's a good habit to get into because I'm only human. I forget things. You don't expect me to be everyone's memory, do you?"

"No. But you are my mother. And I'm not Shelby's.

You should be making supper, not me." I wasn't ready to give up yet, so I slammed the phone down.

It rang again immediately.

"Hello," I said.

"Lizzie, don't you ever —"

I slammed the phone down on my mom, again.

The next few times it rang, I answered and hung up all in one motion. I could have let the answering machine get it but I didn't want to hear her voice at all. She finally gave up.

I made cream of mushroom soup with grilled cheese for supper. Once Shelby was off to her practice, I grabbed an apple, a box of crackers, and a drink — snacks for the evening. Then I locked myself in my room for the night.

Mom grounded me, of course. Not only did I have to miss my soccer game, but she made me phone Vern to tell him I wouldn't be there. Vern didn't freak out on me about it but I knew he would've been disappointed if he knew why, considering how he felt about respect and all. I felt a little embarrassed.

I spent most of the weekend in my bedroom. Whenever Mom called me to eat, I wouldn't go. But when everyone was out of the house, I'd sneak into the kitchen and make myself eggs or soup and load up on snacks for the next stretch of self-imposed exile.

By Sunday night I was bored, bored, bored. I had finished my library books. The radio DJs were no longer sounding cool. I'd listened to the playlist on my iPod enough times to make even the most loyal fan sick of it.

★ ★ ★

Monday morning and school seemed like heaven.

"Where were you?" Alex demanded.

"Grounded," I said.

"So, don't you want to know how we did?" Rosa asked.

"We tanked. There are so many wimps on our team." Alex didn't wait for my response.

"Better not let Vern hear you talk that way," Pam warned.

"Who cares?" Alex asked as she tossed her taffy-coloured hair.

"You would if he benched you," I said.

"His best player? Not likely." She laughed.

"Don't listen to her. We didn't, like, tank. We lost. Okay? Three to nothing. We just had bad luck." Pam waltzed into the math room, straight to our usual seats. A look of confusion spread across her face.

Brock and James weren't sitting there. They had moved to the back of the room and were seated in the middle of a group of boys.

"Yo, Pam." Brock waved her over. He whispered something to the boy seated behind him. The kid nodded, smiled, and gave an exaggerated bow as he offered his seat to her.

Pam looked at me — looked at the vacant chair. When she pleaded with her eyes, I shrugged and nodded consent.

I had told her about my being grounded but not about my misunderstanding with Brock. From the looks of things, I must have really ticked him off.

He kept his distance all week long. Pam sacrificed her happiness and resumed sitting with me after the first day. It felt weird, though, not to have a "cupcake" or "Dizzy-Lizzie" or something coming my way.

Grow up, Lizzie, I told myself. *You can't have it both ways. Either you want him to knock it off or you don't. And you want him to knock it off — right?*

★ ★ ★

Shelby had a soccer game against the Lasers on Saturday morning and, as usual, I went. We were at the Spectrum, so spectator seating was limited. Our fans were squished together at one end.

Brock wasn't there. He had told me he came to all his sister's games. To my surprise, I felt disappointed. It's not like we sat together or talked — we didn't.

"Oh, there's the nice boy who asked about you last week." Mom was waving her arms at Brock, who had just walked in.

The Brock-o-li asked about me? I don't know why but that made me feel good.

My mother scrunched closer to the lady sitting next to her, making room between us for him. It felt strange sitting beside Brock. He hadn't said a word to me. I guess he was still mad about Ms. Oliver's detention. Being polite as ever to adults, though. He had said hi and thanks to my mom. I was relieved once the match started because it gave me something to focus on.

When I watch a game of soccer, strange things happen in me. I'm a mass of tension — it's as if I'm on the pitch. My leg muscles tighten with the kicks our side takes. I strain my upper body muscles as if to capture the loose ball and my tummy tenses in anticipation of the throw-in. I find myself swaying from side to side. The movements are so slight that I'm sure no one can notice anything.

It wasn't long before I forgot the Brock-o-li was there.

Shelby's team was making a run down the pitch. She picked up the ball on an awesome pass from the defence. She then one-timed it to her centre, who sent it into the right corner to the other forward. The forward played the angle off the wall perfectly. The ball bounced back to the centre. She gave it a hard boot. What a save by the goalie! The ball ricocheted off her shin back into the thick of things.

You could cut the tension with a knife. My muscles

were all knotted. I covered my mouth with my hand, holding my breath.

Suddenly, Shelby squeezed between two opponents and connected with the ball. She sent it flying over the goalie's upstretched arms and into the net.

The air whooshed out of my lungs. "*Yes*," I yelled, reaching out to grab Mom.

"Getting friendly?" Brock whispered as I grabbed his leg.

I had totally forgotten he was there. I whipped my hand away as if he were molten metal and my face went beet red.

"S ... s ... sorry," I stammered.

"No problem." The Brock-o-li laughed. "This game's sure starting out exciting, isn't it?"

All I could trust myself to do was nod.

By the second half, Shelby's team was up eight to nothing. I found I had relaxed a bit. But they didn't let up, they just kept racking up the score. It was twelve to nothing by the fifteen-minute mark. The Lasers' goalie looked defeated and she took a swipe at her eyes. Was she crying or was she just wiping sweat off her face?

Our side made another run for the goal but lost the ball to an opposing player.

Behind me a father yelled. "What's with you, kid? You just coughed up the ball to a do-nothing team. Wake up already!"

I found myself pulling for the Lasers as they took

the ball up the pitch. I felt like a traitor, but I couldn't help myself because I tend to pull for underdogs. I usually am the underdog. So when the ball dribbled in on a shot screened by our centre, I cheered.

"Hey, kid, what team are you for?" the man behind me muttered.

"Jerk. Like it's really going to matter now," Brock whispered to me.

But it did matter to the Lasers. The way they hooted and high-fived, you would have thought they had won the game. And it seemed to matter to Shelby's coach because he screamed at the girl who had screened the goalie.

Our girls took to the pitch with renewed determination and got two more quick goals.

"You'd think the coach would tell our girls to hold back. The other team can't hope to catch up," I said.

"He's got no class. You should have seen the American roller-hockey team when they played Paraguay in the Pan Am Games. Now they were classy. They refused to humiliate the opposition. They held the score at six to nothing, but they still showed their skill. Their stickhandling and checking was awesome. No running up the score for them. That's sportsmanship." Brock nodded.

I looked at him in surprise because that was the kind of thing Vern would have said.

* * *

"That soccer game was something else, eh Lizzie?" Brock dropped into the seat in front of me.

"You were, like, at our game? It was a squeaker wasn't it? Too bad we lost." Pam was grinning from ear to ear as she stood beside my desk. She gave me a friendly push. "Lizzie, why didn't you tell me Brock was there?"

"Because he wasn't." I hated to burst her bubble. "He's talking about Shelby's game."

"Why would you go to her game?" Pam asked Brock.

"Ashley plays on the same team," he answered.

"Oh..."

Pam was still standing beside me when Henchel walked in. "Lizzie," she whispered through her teeth.

I didn't move. I pretended I didn't hear because I didn't need her to sit between Brock and me anymore.

She slipped into the seat behind me.

Pam was angry. I could feel her seething all morning and at lunchtime she let me have it.

"How long has this been going on? The two of you going to Shelby's games together?"

"You're nuts," I shot back. "I go to see my sister and he goes to see his. We don't go together."

"Then why didn't you tell me? Why keep it a secret?"

"I wasn't trying to. It never occurred to me to tell you."

"You should've told me, okay? A best friend would

have let her friend know that she saw *the man of her friend's dreams* at a soccer game."

Maybe she was right, but the thought had never entered my mind.

10 SOUR GRAPES

"Your team's playing up in the Snickers' Tournament? In our division? That's awful!" I pushed Shelby's arm away from me. The new uniform that she was holding out for me to admire slipped from her hand. The offending red outfit irritated me like a cape waved before a bull.

"I thought you'd be happy," Shelby whispered, retrieving the shorts and shirt.

"Why would I be? Play against little kids? Compete with my baby sister? I thought I left that behind with elementary school."

Tears welled up in her eyes. "I thought it would be fun," she said.

"Well, I don't. It's the stupidest thing I've ever heard." I stamped my foot.

"That's enough, Lizzie," my mother said. She wrapped her arms around Shelby.

"But Mom, why can't they play in their own level?"

"They're cleaning everybody's clocks in division

102

nine. It's not good to have a team that's so mismatched with the rest of the division."

"So they move up and spoil our tournament?"

"It shouldn't spoil anything. I'm told they do this all the time, Lizzie. Shelby's coach needs to know if the team is capable of playing at a higher level before he moves them up next season."

"You mean during the regular games?"

"Well ... yes."

"That's not fair to us."

"Why not? You're just jealous our team's hot," Shelby finally spoke, her hurt feelings turning to anger.

"No! Of course not." She was wrong, I knew it, but I couldn't explain why yet.

I was in a black mood as I dressed for soccer practice. For the last three years I've played in the Snickers' Tournament. Every year Mom and Dad hemmed and hawed about letting me play. They felt it took up too much of the holidays. It's played between Boxing Day and New Year's. In the end, they always gave in.

This time it was different. When Vern had phoned to ask if I wanted to play, they had said yes right away.

Even though I no longer believed in the magic of the uniforms, this year still felt lucky. I believed in our team. We were doing well and were in the top half of the pack. I believed we could win the tournament as long as The Big Three kept playing up.

Shelby's news changed everything. It wasn't that

I even considered that they might win; it just took the shine off things. It also explained why my parents hadn't given me a hard time about taking part in the tournament.

★ ★ ★

"All right, what's all the complaining about? We haven't even started yet. After stretching, warm-up, and some laps — then you can grouse." Vern tossed a couple of soccer balls towards where we were huddled.

We all started to talk at once.

"You know what the coach from division nine is doing?"

"The jerk's putting his little kids in our division."

"He's got them new uniforms."

"Red. They're not even River Park colours. We've always been green."

"I'll be playing my younger sister!"

"Okay, ladies, I can see you're quite upset. Maybe we should take some time to vent." He squatted to be closer to our level. "Let me get this straight — you're upset because the division nine team is playing against us in the tournament?"

Most of us nodded.

He scratched the back of his neck, pursed his lips and shook his head. "I seem to recall some mighty happy people when I told you The Big Three were playing up. Do I detect some hypocrisy here?"

"No, but —"

"But what? That benefited you and this doesn't?" he interrupted, not pulling any punches.

"This is different," I said.

"How?" he challenged.

I'd been thinking about it since Shelby had accused me of being jealous. I'd figured out what was bothering me and talking with the other girls had made it even clearer.

"The way I see it is this. The Big Three were junior high girls moving up to play against other junior high girls. We're being expected to play against elementary kids," I explained.

"And that's a problem?"

"Well, yeah," I continued. "Who wants to play against little kids when you're in junior high? You keep telling us to play aggressively. How can we? The school tells us it's our responsibility to look after the elementary students. To be gentle and kind with them."

"Lizzie's right, y'know," Pam said. "We're teenagers. Well, almost, okay? We're expected to, like, act grown up around them."

"No kidding," Jen agreed. Her curly blond ponytail bobbed as she nodded. "Some of us babysit those kids, for goodness sake. When we play with them, we let them win."

"It's not just at school either." Maxie's grey eyes

flashed. "My mom is always yelling at me for being too rough when I horse around with my little brother and sister. It's not like I'm doing it on purpose. I can't help being big for my age." She sighed and ran her fingers through her dark curls.

"How'd you like to be me?" Angie complained. "I'll be playing against my sister in grade six."

"That team's not just grade sixes. My sister's on the team, too, and she's only in grade five. There are lots of ten-year-olds on that team," I added.

"You guys are such wimps. Afraid of being beaten by elementary kids," Alex sneered.

"Yeah, I'd hate to lose for real to younger kids. What of it?" Jen said.

"It's more than just that. I've lost to my sister lots of times. Indoor soccer is rough — especially along the boards. I want to play my best and I won't. I know I'll be holding back because I'm playing with little kids."

"Well, I'm not holding back. I've always played against smaller kids. If they think they can play in the big leagues, well, come on up. I'll take them on." Alex sat up straight, accentuating her height.

"You would," I whispered under my breath.

Vern sighed and nodded his head. "I hear ya. What I'm getting is, it's not playing up that you're objecting to but the loss of grown-up status — the indignity of being lumped in with little kids again."

"Yeah."

"It's a tough call, girls. Once in a while we get these extraordinary teams. Their skills are way above their age level. They cream the teams they play. They always win, so they seldom learn the art of losing gracefully. That's sad. They deserve to play at their skill level, to be able to grow. So the system moves them up."

"Yeah, but what about us? Our feelings? Are we only there to provide talented kids with growing experiences?" I said. My belief that average people were always forgotten was strengthened.

"I'm not sure what the answer is, ladies, but I know whining's not going to change anything, is it? So you might as well make the most of what you've got, like soccer and me. Let's get to work."

We hid our disappointment in boos and hisses at Vern's drills, but we worked our butts off because we all knew a trophy was at stake.

★ ★ ★

"See, Lizzie, your fears of having to play Shelby are needless." Mom pointed to the schedule in her hand. "You're in different conferences."

There are two conferences in the Snickers' Tournament. You play a round robin with the other teams in your conference. Officials analyze the win-loss stats to get the top two teams. These teams then move on to the semifinals.

"So which one of our teams do you not expect to make the finals? I bet I can guess," I shot back. I was sick of hearing about how good Shelby's team was. It was the talk of the community. They were even wished good luck over the intercom at school.

Mom's face reddened. "For heaven's sake, Lizzie, I hadn't even thought that far. I was just thinking of your feelings."

"Yeah right," I said, and fled to my room.

I flopped onto my bed. Folding my arms under my head, I stared at the ceiling. There is no way anyone can put a positive spin on this, I thought. They all tried, though — Mom, Dad, and even Vern.

I rolled over and turned on the radio. The carols put me in the mood to wrap my remaining gifts. I always managed to put things off. It was Christmas Eve and I still had some to place under the tree.

Shelby barged into my room.

"Don't you ever knock?" I snarled, not because I was mad, but because she almost saw her present.

"I'm sorry, Lizzie. Can I still sleep here tonight?"

Ever since we were little, Shelby slept over in my room on Christmas Eve. I don't know how it started, but now it was a tradition.

"Of course. Why'd you even think you had to ask?"

"Because of soccer. Because you were mad."

"But that has nothing to do with Christmas," I said. "Now leave, so I can wrap your gift."

I finished my wrapping and went downstairs to join the family. We curled up together to watch Christmas shows, another family tradition.

At eleven-thirty, Mom sent us to bed.

It took us a while to fall asleep. We drifted off, whispering and giggling.

★ ★ ★

Shelby kicked me awake. "It's time. We can wake Mom and Dad." I squinted sleepily at the clock on my bedside table. Seven-thirty. I rolled to face her, but she was gone. I bounced out of bed and down the hall, nearly bumping into Dad. "Need my coffee," he mumbled.

In our family, we unwrap the gifts one at a time, oohing and aahing over each item. I watched as Shelby pulled the paper off her last package.

"Oh, Mom, Dad, thanks!" Shelby's green eyes sparkled as she clutched the shoes to her chest.

"I'm glad you like them, sweetie. After all, your coach insists that you kids should have them." Mom reached out and patted my sister's shoulder.

Indoor soccer shoes — something I had wanted for two years. I was green with envy but I kept my mouth shut. It was Christmas, after all. Something must have given me away, though, or maybe Mom was feeling guilty?

"Lizzie, I know this is something you've wanted.

But Vern has always said they're not necessary. Shelby's coach, on the other hand, frowns on those wearing ordinary sneakers because of the team's superior skill level. We really had no choice," Mom tried to explain.

I shrugged. "Whatever." It really didn't matter what she said, this was another case of those who have getting some more.

She handed me my last gift. I opened it slowly, not caring what was in it. A cell phone! My own phone — I had been begging for one all year. But even though I knew this was a way cooler present, a part of me still longed for those shoes.

11 STEWING

Crawling into a cold car at seven-fifteen in the morning on Boxing Day would be most people's idea of torture, but for me it was heaven. I was going to my first game of the Snickers' Tournament. Shelby's game was right after mine, so the whole family was in the car. Mom was going to get to see me play, finally.

I had to get my mind off Shelby's new soccer shoes. I stared at the sneakers on my lap. My lucky runners. With my fingers, I followed their contours. The old things had served me well. They had molded themselves to my feet and had helped me kick in my goals. Maybe if I got a few more, that would do it.

We pulled into the winter club's parking lot. The soccer complex was one of those inflated domes. They set it up on the outdoor tennis courts during the winter. We kids loved to chase each other in the revolving doors that lead to the pitch — it drove the adults crazy. While the parents got coffee from the vending machine, a number of us kids took advantage of being unsupervised for a few minutes.

"Knock it off, ladies. You'll make yourselves sick." Vern held the door from moving.

I staggered out laughing and followed him to our change room.

"Get out there as quick as you can to warm up, girls," Vern said as he headed toward our bench.

Our first game was against the Terriers. It was a good way to start because we were evenly matched. We'd played them a couple of times already this season, winning one and losing one, so it was anybody's game as long as you worked hard.

The whistle blew to start the game. Vern usually started Alex at centre and Maxie on her right so we'd have power out there until we found our rhythm. I got to play left forward on their line.

Alex passed across to right forward while I made a break down the left. Maxie booted directly onto my foot. I deked around the defence, hoofing the ball at the back wall. It ricocheted into the box, straight in line with the goal. Alex stopped it. She couldn't get a shot off. So passed it back to me. I kicked for the net. It bounced off the goalie, hit the side of the goal, and dribbled in.

Not a pretty goal, I thought, but hey, we'll take it.

It was one of those crazy games where everything went our way. The weak shots dribbled in while great saves by their goalie resulted in rebounds for us. When our shots caught the edge of the goal, they fell in, not out. The Terriers had as many chances as we did, but their shots hit the sides of the goal, bounced off players, went anywhere but in. Our four-to-nothing victory belied the fact that it was a hard-fought match played by equals.

Shelby's game was another thing altogether. When the two teams took to the field it looked like David and Goliath — and Goliath was going to win. The Jazz came out fighting. They were a tough team that played hard, played rough. Made up of mostly large girls, this team forced you to struggle for everything you got. You had to out-finesse them.

Shelby's team looked as though they didn't stand a chance. Right off the bat one of their players got a ball in the face and went off with a bloody nose. When play resumed, the Jazz made a run for the goal. Their centre hoofed it hard at the net.

Shelby's keeper made a beautiful save but her fingers bent back when stopping the speeding ball and the coach had to replace her.

"Hey, you meatheads. Feeling real big injuring grade school kids, eh?" a man yelled. It was the same obnoxious fan from Shelby's last game.

The little kids were being flung around like straws in the wind. Someone's going to get hurt badly, I thought. In my disgust at having to play against elementary kids, this had not occurred to me before.

A few minutes later, one of the grade fives had the wind knocked out of her. She'd collided with the Jazz's left defence as she tried to deke around the larger kid.

"Hey, girly. Yeah, you. You should be ashamed of yourself picking on a ten-year-old," the loudmouth from the stands yelled again.

The player from the Jazz took a closer look at the injured kid. She raised her hand to her mouth, looking sheepish, as the little girl was helped off the ground. You could tell she felt badly.

The whistle blew to resume play, but something had changed. The Jazz that was on the pitch wasn't the same Jazz that started the game. Oh, they played strongly when they had the ball, got some nice goals on hard shots, but they never seemed to challenge when Shelby's team had the ball. In the end it cost them — they lost by a goal.

Brock walked up to us after the game. I hadn't seen him anywhere when the match started. Pam and I had looked. She'd gone home with her dad when we couldn't find him.

"What a game!" he said.

"Weren't our little guys awesome?" my mother gushed back.

If Shelby had said that, I probably would have said yes, but I figured Mom and Brock could take the truth. "They did okay. But the Jazz had an off game. If they were on, they'd have walked all over Shelby's team."

"Yeah, like you're an expert. Admit it, those little kids are good." Brock laughed.

"I didn't say they weren't. But so are the Jazz. They're not the top team in our division for nothing." I looked for Dad to back me up. He had seen the Jazz play. But he'd gone to warm up the car.

"Lizzie, those little kids played their hearts out. Give credit where credit is due," Mom said.

"I thought I was. Maybe you should do the same," I snapped back. I was tired of hearing how good Shelby's team was. "I've played the Jazz. You've never even seen them before. They're aggressive and so are a few of the other teams. Someone on Shelby's team is going to get hurt. You wait and see."

"Stop being melodramatic, Lizzie. It's just a kid's game, not the big leagues."

Brock looked at us in surprise. He stood there uncomfortably for a moment, then said, "I'd better go."

"Now, look, we've embarrassed the poor boy," Mom said.

I watched him walk over to a lady in a wheelchair. She had to be a relative. Although her back was to us the red-orange hair was a dead give away. Brock leaned down and whispered something to her. She burst out in one of those laughs that draws you in, even if you don't know what the joke's about. It sets you on a roller coaster ride of giggles that leaves you weak but satisfied, that is, if you're not the brunt of the joke and I was sure

I was. At that moment I disliked both her and Brock intensely.

"Well, people shouldn't jump to conclusions," I snapped in reply to my mother. "Just because Shelby's team kills all the others in their division, doesn't mean they can do it in ours."

"No. But I'm sure they're competitive. Her coach thinks so."

"Good for him." I stalked off to go wait in the car.

"So, Lizzie." Brock elbowed me in the side as Shelby's team racked up another win. They'd made a clean sweep of their conference. "What do you have to say about this game? The Blues had a bad day, too?"

I let it go. There was no way I could win this one. Shelby's team had played an excellent match, out-muscling the older girls. They were the better of the two, but the Blues were at the bottom of our division in the regular season. If I even hinted at that, no one would believe me. I had learned to shut up after Shelby's second victory.

"See, dear? They're fair contenders. This proves you're wrong," my mom had said.

What she didn't understand was the word had gotten out that Shelby's team was made up of little kids. No one likes to hurt little kids, so that made a difference in the way their opponents played. I knew that to be true since I'd seen it with my own eyes and I knew I would have backed off, too.

The adults in the know saw the difference also. I overheard the Jazz's coach talking to Vern as we got ready to play our last game.

"I hear the River Park's division nine girls are really cleaning up. They're that good?" Vern asked.

"They're good for their age, no doubt about it. They should be giving the average teams a good fight. Maybe winning a couple. But coming out on top? Honestly? I don't think so," the other man answered.

"So? What gives?"

"Darned if I know. I thought my girls eased up because of the injuries that team took. But that wasn't it. When playing the little ones, injuries or no injuries, all the other teams were off their games. They seemed to have lost their aggression, lost their drive."

"Don't they get it? The players back off because the kids are little, not just because someone got hurt." I whispered, elbowing Pam and wagging my head in their direction.

"Anyone on our team could have told them that would happen." She nodded in agreement.

"But they aren't asking us, are they? And if we say anything we're accused of being jealous," I complained.

"You too?" asked Angie. "I thought I was the only one having that thrown in my face. I quit going to my sister's games. That way I couldn't comment on how the teams played. I'd just say 'That's nice,' whenever Mom told me they won.'"

Vern's laughter caught my attention again. "Boohoo. The other teams didn't back off for your team. They made you work for second place, did they?"

"Heck yeah. Except for the games with that one squad, it's been a tight tournament." The Jazz's coach laughed too, waved and left.

We'd won three and lost one in the round robin so far. The Terriers and Lightning had done the same. If we were to move on, we had to win this game and one of the other two teams needed to lose.

We took to the pitch pumped but tense.

The Thunder kicked off a long boot across the pitch. Their forward captured the ball and dribbled it down the field. I stopped her along the boards and tried to steal it, but no luck. It wouldn't budge no matter how many times I kicked — or how hard. Then when I least expected it, out it popped. It bounced towards Pam. She sent it back to me. I kicked, barely connecting. But Alex got to it before the Thunder's player. She muscled her way over the centre, then hoofed it to Maxie. I got myself open to wait for the rebound. Maxie booted the ball. It went hard off the wall — and right to me. I kicked for the left corner. Robbed, just great! The goalie got a piece of the ball. It bounced to the Thunder defence and she kicked it up the field. I headed for the bench for a line change.

By halftime, it was still zero to zero.

"Well, ladies. I saw some good things out there this half. You're touching the ball. You're using the wall to your advantage. The passing's great, and you're sticking with your men. So far so good. But you're still waiting for the other side to make the moves when they have the ball."

"But Vern, they haven't scored yet either." Rosa brushed a wisp of dark hair off her face.

"Do you want to win this game or not, ladies?"

We nodded.

"I can't hear you." Vern cupped his ear with his hand.

"Yes."

"What?"

"*Yes!*"

"All right, then we've got to force the play. Make our own breaks."

The ref blew his whistle. We got up and huddled. "*Go, Pythons, Go!*"

"Okay, ladies, go out there and turn it up a notch."

The Thunder's coach must have pumped them up also, because they came out flying. Neither team could get the advantage. We just went up and down the pitch. Alex started to get mad. Usually that's a good sign because she goes into bulldog mode and often scores. This time, however, she just kept losing the ball and getting angrier. Vern called her to come off. She pretended she didn't hear and continued going for the ball. Her energy ran out and a Thunder player with fresh legs forced her to cough up the ball. She deked past our defence and pumped one off the wall to their centre, who one-timed the ball at our net. Jen dove for it. Got a piece, but not enough. In it went.

"Nice try, Jen. Let go of it, ladies. You've got six minutes to get it back. Lots of time," Vern called from the bench.

We went on the offensive. But no matter what we did, the ball wouldn't go in the Thunder's net. The whistle blew. We had run out of time.

Waves of disappointment washed over me. I saw Jen rub a tear from her face. I felt weepy too, but I wasn't going to cry.

"Great game, ladies, you did all the right things. I guess it just wasn't our turn." Vern patted Jen's back. "Go home and enjoy the rest of the holidays. We'll resume practices on the second Thursday after New Year's."

I grabbed my things and headed for the stands.

"What a relief that's over. I was dreading a River Park playoff," I heard Angie's mom saying to my mom. She pulled a woolen hat over her fading rusty hair.

"No kidding. Could you imagine anything so —"

"Awful?" I cut off Mom's reply. My disappointment had turned to anger. "What loyalty — our own parents pulling for us to lose."

"Lizzie, stop it."

But I couldn't stop myself. "What, Mom? Thought I didn't know? All along everyone's wanted my perfect little sister's team to clean up in my tournament."

"That's enough." Mom tried to lead me from the Gateway soccer complex, but I fought back, forcing her to drag me out of the building. "We were talking about how heart-wrenching it's been for us parents. What you did was just too rude. I expect better of you, Lizzie."

"Well, I expect better of you too, Mom." My tears started to fall.

"You've got it wrong, all wrong, honey. It's not that we wanted your team to lose. But Shelby's team had already topped their conference. A River Park final would be a no-win proposition. Who would I have pulled for?"

"But this is my sport. I've played it since grade four. Shelby only played to copy me —" I swiped at my tears.

"I know, sweetie." Mom put her arms around me. "You, Lizzie, have a zest for life. You take big chomps out of the world around you and savour every bite. You'll make the world your oyster. I'll never have to worry about you, but I do worry about Shelby. Your sister is so fickle about things, even when she does them well. For the first time she's sticking to something — and enjoying it. I can't help pulling for that, Lizzie."

"Why can't you pull for good soccer? Cheer for whoever does something well. Let the best team win. Is that so hard?"

"Yes, because in the end one of my little girls has to lose to the other."

"Then maybe Shelby's team shouldn't have been moved up."

"It really doesn't matter now, does it?" She swayed gently, rocking me.

12 BITTER FRUIT

But it did matter. The Terriers lost their game too, and because we had beaten them, we placed first. *Yes*.

I was looking forward to Mom seeing the Jazz in action against us. Then she'd have to admit that they were a better team than the one she saw. But they scheduled the semifinal matches at the same time and in different complexes.

"Well, ladies, we made it in by the skin of our teeth. We were given a lucky break. Now let's get out there, use our skills, and make our own breaks."

The Jazz were back and they were fighting mad.

"First we'll crush you. And if your rugrats win today, we'll stomp them next. It's our trophy," their left forward hissed as we struggled along the wall.

The ball popped away from us. Their centre picked it up and was gone. I took off after the play. Maxie cut her off, forcing a pass. Alex intercepted it and took the play right down the centre in the other direction. The Jazz defence challenged, and the play was back in our end. Jen grabbed the ball as it rolled into the box and punted it to me. I got a piece of it with my foot, directing it to Pam as she changed on the fly. Then I headed for the bench myself, beat.

By my second shift the Jazz had become chippy. A lot of raised elbows accompanied the usual bump and grind along the boards. Small players, like Pam and Rosa, found themselves flat on their butts when the ref wasn't looking. The game was played in our end with increasing frequency as more Pythons limped off to nurse their wounds.

"They're out-muscling us, ladies. It's been Jen's awesome goaltending that has kept us in the game," Vern said at halftime. He wasn't telling us anything we didn't know already.

"You're a gutsy team. You can out-finesse them. I've seen you do it. Don't back off when the Jazz get rough — make them take the foul. Now go out there and smoke 'em."

His pep talk fired us up. We managed to keep the play in their end as much as they did in ours, but none of our shots on net were getting past their goalie. Then we got a lucky break. Maxie hoofed the ball. Their defender raised her arms to protect her face from the speeding projectile — handball, just within the box.

Alex took the penalty kick. One on one, her size alone usually intimidated goalies, but not this keeper, who was almost as tall and solid muscle. They stared each other down for a moment. Then Alex made her move, a beautiful boot in the upper left corner. The other girl didn't stand a chance.

We went wild. But our joy was short-lived as the Jazz got the goal back on the very next play. The tie held until the whistle blew.

"Okay, ladies. Nobody likes a game to be decided on sudden death penalty kicks, but that's how it's done in tournaments. Goalie against the shooter. That's all. Their keeper is big and strong but not very agile, so kick for the corners. Alex, you shoot first. If it goes in — great. If not, Maxie's next, followed by Angie." Vern listed us off in the order of our kicking ability. "Jen, you just keep on playing like you have. You've been awesome. Good luck, ladies."

The Jazz centre kicked first. A lovely shot. Jen's save was lovelier.

"Go, girl." Rosa patted Alex's back as she passed.

"All right. Let's put this game away," she said as she headed to the net.

The Pythons gave her the thumbs up.

What were the chances of Alex repeating her last goal? One in a million? That's why we stood there stunned when it went in.

"Well? Where's my cheering section?" she demanded as she returned to the bench. We swarmed her, high-fiving and hugging.

"Okay. Enough of this. On to the finals." Alex beamed.

★ ★ ★

I guess it was Mom's worst nightmare come to life — Shelby and I facing each other in the playoffs. She'd avoided the topic all afternoon. When we got to the Spectrum she just waved to us and called good luck as we headed to our separate change rooms. She seemed a million miles away sitting there in the stands. It was easy to pick her out from our bench, as she was the only mom in a fur coat. Brock was right, she did look like a model. For the first time I saw her as someone other than my mom. I could even sympathize with her, but that didn't stop me from wanting to win the game.

I shifted my gaze to Shelby. She looked so tiny lining up on the field across from Maxie. She's going to get hurt, I thought.

"Why can't the adults, like, see how dangerous this is?" Pam echoed my thoughts.

"There's no way I'm going to feel comfortable muscling them around, especially my own sister. She'll go crying to Mom," Angie shook her head.

It was obvious the rest of our team felt the same. We addressed the ball when it came our way. Our passes were strong and our use of the wall was good, but we weren't being aggressive. We weren't challenging them at all along the boards or when they controlled the ball. Time and time again they set up plays and made a run for the goal. If it wasn't for Alex, they would never have lost possession at all. True to her word, she treated them like any other team.

"For heaven's sake, guys, we're being outplayed by elementary kids." Alex shook her head in disgust, trying to motivate us.

We ignored her and relied on Jen to keep us in the game. But when you're facing a shooting gallery, sooner or later one is going to go in. When it did, a roar of cheers filled the building, drowning out our groans and the halftime buzzer.

"Ladies, what can I say? It's brutal out there. Where's the spunk? The determination? Where are my girls? And who is this team wearing our uniforms?"

"Y'know, Vern, we warned you this would happen," Pam said.

"No, no, no. No excuses. You're a team. You're letting down your goalie. If you really want to win you're going to have to get over the nice-ies and give those little kids the game they came for."

"No kidding. Are we just going to hand them the trophy? Come on, you guys, I'm not saying we go out there and beat them up. Just make them earn the spot in our division. Okay?" Alex pleaded.

"*Right on.*" Vern high-fived her.

I took my place on the left side of Alex when the whistle blew for the second half. You could hear a pin drop as we waited for the kickoff.

"Hey, Lizzie. Is your team having an off game, too?" Brock's voice echoed in the silence.

I wanted to smack that smug smiling face. He made my blood boil — made me determined to play my best. When the ball came my way, I muscled it away from their forward and booted it to Rosa. She picked it up on the fly and passed it across to Alex, who kicked it towards the goal. The goalie caught it and punted it back up the field. It arced towards me. I swung my leg hard to meet it in mid-air. *Thwack.* My foot connected with something soft. It wasn't the ball. Angie had headed it just before it got to me. *Thud.* Something hit the boards hard.

For a moment time stood still. Then a scream and the ref's whistle sounded as one. I turned to look. A figure lay crumpled on the ground along the wall near the bleachers. People were running. The coach and manager from Shelby's team dashed across the field. Dad was leaning over the boards. I saw Mom teeter down the stands in her high-heeled boots, a hand over her mouth. Brock was helping her.

Shelby! I started to run. The ref grabbed me.

"Go sit down on the field," he said, releasing me.

As soon as he let go of me, I tried to get to my sister. He grabbed me again. I struggled to get away.

"Get her out of here," he yelled.

I felt Vern's arm on my shoulder. "Come on, Lizzie. There's nothing you can do. Let them do their job."

I let him lead me to the bench.

Through my tears I watched the ambulance attendants take my sister away on a stretcher. My mom and dad trailed behind.

The ref walked over to our bench. "Number ten's out of the game. Intent to injure."

"Are you kidding? It was an accident." Vern shook his head.

"That's not the way I saw it. The ball wasn't near her when she kicked that kid."

"But it was going her way. It just didn't get there. It was intercepted in flight."

"That's your opinion. I saw it different. I've made my call."

"Fine." Vern's light brown eyes smouldered and he shook his head again. "Rosa, take the penalty."

"No, it's not fine," Alex said. "Where does he get off making that kind of call? It was an accident. Anyone with half a brain could see that."

The ref turned and walked away.

"Alex. Get back here," Vern called as she jumped over the boards and followed the referee. "Alex. Alex ... "

She ignored him.

"That was her sister. Why would she try and hurt her own kid sister? Answer me that for heaven's sake!" Alex grabbed the ref's arm.

"I really don't care what their relationship is. I'm warning you, kid, get back to your bench." He wrenched his arm from Alex's grasp, then blew his whistle to resume the game.

But Alex wouldn't let up. "Are you blind? That little kid came out of nowhere. You should have seen that she came out of nowhere."

The referee flashed a red card in Alex's face. "Get her off the pitch," he ordered.

Vern dragged Alex off the field. "Coach, please? You can't just let him do that."

"Alex, go sit there quietly," Vern said firmly. He pointed to the far corner of the box where I was. "And Alex, you're benched next game of regular play. You've cost us. Now we have to play two men short for the next five minutes."

The ref was really ticked. He gave us a delay-of-game penalty, too.

Even if the ref hadn't thrown me out of the game, I wouldn't have been capable of playing. The tears just kept flowing as I sobbed silently. *Shelby, please be okay,* I prayed.

"Look, it was an accident." Alex put her arm around my shoulder. "I tried to tell the ref that. But the idiot wouldn't listen. The next thing I know, he's red carding me too. And then what does Vern do? He benches me. Go figure."

I was grateful that Alex had stood up for me, but I understood where Vern was coming from — the way he felt about respect and all.

"Hey, Pam's got a breakaway. Look at her move. Go, girl! Get this one for Lizzie. Yes, yes, yes." Alex was standing now.

I didn't bother. The game held no interest for me. It didn't matter that my best friend had just scored. Nor did I care that the little kids were shying away from our players and letting us walk in and score. We had racked up five goals in as many minutes. Vern told us to hold back and play a defensive game only. It made no difference, the little ones were only going through the motions.

When the buzzer sounded, their coach stormed up to Vern. "Keep that vicious kid away from my girls. Look what she's done to my team. Broken their spirits." His pointing finger jabbed in my direction. "We don't need the likes of her in the sport. This is supposed to be a friendly game."

"Come on, now. It was an accident —"

"Like hell." He pushed away Vern's extended hand and refused to shake it.

"Go on out there and shake their hands. You did nothing wrong," Vern insisted.

On the field our team was quietly hugging each other. I wanted no part of it but I did as I was told. I pumped hands and let the tournament officials put the medal around my neck. But as soon as I could, I escaped to the change room.

13 WAKE UP AND SMELL THE COFFEE

"How're you getting home? Do you need a ride?" Vern asked as he herded us out.

I looked at him blankly. I hadn't even thought of that. "I'd better stay. I'm sure my parents will come back for me."

Ever since I was small my mom and dad had said, "If you're lost, stay put. We'll find you." I knew I wasn't lost but I figured the same rule applied. They wouldn't just leave me there.

"Okay, I'll wait with you."

As we stood by the entrance, Vern kept looking at his watch. Finally he said, "I've got to be somewhere important in ten minutes. Let me drive you home."

"I can't. They'll expect me to be here," I insisted.

"I can't leave you here alone."

"Sir, if you have to go, I'll wait with her." Brock was standing by the pro-shop door.

"Who's he? Do you know him?" Vern asked.

"Brock's in my class at school. You go. I'll be safe

with him," I said.

"I don't know…You sure you won't let me take you home?"

I shook my head.

"Well, I can't stay any longer…"

As soon as Vern left, Brock led me to the coffee shop. "Sit at that table. You can watch the front entrance from there. I'll go get us drinks."

"Why were you still hanging around? Why didn't you go home with your family?" I asked as he handed me a cola.

"My parents weren't here. They're at work. When they can't come, my sister gets a ride with the coach and waits at the neighbours till I get home. I take a bus."

"Couldn't you get a ride with him, too?"

"Wouldn't want to. I don't like the man."

"I'm glad," I said. He gave me this strange look. "Oh, no, I don't mean I'm glad you dislike the man. I'm just glad you were here to wait with me."

He smiled. We sat quietly sipping our drinks. It sure was good not to be alone.

"Weird game, huh?" Brock broke the silence.

"I didn't mean to kick her." I bristled.

"Hey, calm down, I didn't say you did. Shelby came from behind. Squeezed between you and the boards. You know? Like she always does."

"Tell that to the ref," I sighed.

"Yeah. Too bad he had his back turned to you. He

was pretty shook up. Everyone was. I guess he felt the need to do something to make himself feel in control of the situation."

"I don't really care. I just want to go home. I want to know how Shelby is. I wish my parents would get here." My tears started to flow again.

" Oh, crap. Please don't start crying. I'm sure they'll be here soon."

But they weren't. An hour passed. Brock bought us each another pop.

"Maybe you should call home," he pushed a cell phone across the table.

"They won't be home. They wouldn't forget me."

"Not normally, but what happened today isn't normal. Call one of their cells."

"See? I told you, no answer." My lips started to quiver. I gulped back my tears. "Shelby must be really badly hurt. I want to go home. Now."

"Okay. We'll take the next bus." He looked at his watch. "Come on, we have to run. The bus will be here any minute. They only come every half-hour."

We reached the stop just as the bus pulled up.

"Here." Brock handed me a ticket. "Don't forget to take a transfer."

I don't think I could have made it home if he hadn't been there. We had to change buses twice. He was going to get off and see me to the door, too, but I wouldn't let him. He would have had to walk home then.

I was still jiggling my key in the door when Mom and Dad pulled up. I ran towards the car, but stopped before I got there. The back seat was empty.

"Ooh ... Shelby. I knew this would happen, Mom. I said someone was going to get hurt. You wouldn't listen. You should have listened." I pounded my fists on the car.

"Lizzie, Lizzie. Shelby's okay, sweetie." Mom put her arms around me and hugged me close. "They're just keeping her at the hospital overnight, for observation."

I burst out crying, tears of relief, tears of anger.

"How could you forget to pick me up?" I bawled.

"Didn't Shelby's coach bring you home? He told us to both go with Shelby. He said he'd bring you home."

"Well, I guess he forgot. He was so angry after the game, he stormed off without shaking hands."

"That doesn't sound right. Are you sure, Lizzie?" asked Dad.

"It's true, ask Vern. Their coach got so mad because Shelby's team lost. They fell apart after she got hurt. He called me vicious. He said I did it on purpose. Do you think I did it on purpose, too?"

"Of course not, Lizzie. It was an accident. He had no right to call you that." Dad slammed the car door shut.

"So who drove you home?" Mom asked.

"No one. Brock got me home. He waited with me. When you didn't come, we took the bus. He does it all the time so he can watch his sister play. We should give him a ride from now on. It took us three buses to get home from the Spectrum, I wonder how many it takes from Gateway." I was babbling but I couldn't stop myself. Then all my pent up tension broke loose and I started to shake.

"Aaron, let's take her inside. She's freezing, poor kid."

I sat on the sofa, wrapped in a blanket, but I was still shivering slightly. Dad sat down beside me and put his arm around me.

"Here, maybe this will help." Mom handed me the mug of hot chocolate she had just made. She then dropped onto the chair beside us. "What a day. I never want to go through this again."

"I'm sorry. I'm sor—" I started sniffing again.

"Oh, honey, I'm not blaming you." She reached over and patted my leg. "You did nothing wrong. To think I was worried about how I was going to console the girl who lost the soccer game and at the same time be happy for the winner. This sure puts things into perspective."

"No kidding. You put your kids in sports for a million positive reasons, but you never think about them being injured — until it happens." Dad picked up his mug and took a sip.

"Well, in this case you should have." I couldn't help myself. I needed to get things off my chest. "I know everyone thought that I was just jealous when I said it was a bad idea. But that first game Shelby played against the Jazz — when the kids were being tossed around — people should have noticed."

"But they won."

"Only because the Jazz pulled back. Dad, didn't you figure that out?"

"I guess, like everyone else, I was wearing blinders."

"Honey, we were all so proud of those little guys that we saw what we wanted to see. We believed they won on talent because they always won. The way things turned out..." Mom shook her head and closed her eyes for a moment. "You were right, Lizzie. Oh lord, you were right."

They let Shelby come home the next morning. She had a goose egg the size of a golf ball on the back of her head. An ugly bluish-purple bruise spread up and across her right cheek from under her chin, where I had kicked her. There was no concussion, thank goodness. Every time I looked at her I felt guilty and angry. I was angry at adults who only looked at skill levels and ignored body size. Why didn't they care about our feelings? Why did they only care about winning? Why didn't they listen to our warnings? Mom and Dad finally understood what I was getting at. Too bad Shelby had to pay for their mistake first. But Shelby wasn't the only one paying.

★ ★ ★

Our team was huddled together in a corner of the room, discussing the fallout from our victory. It was our first practice since the holidays. All week long the kids at school had been calling us names like bullies and baby-beaters.

"Well, ladies? What are you plotting? Your next victory, I hope." Vern's voice boomed in the quiet gym.

We didn't answer him.

Vern dropped the sports bag he was carrying and took off his jacket. A number of parents drifted in from the front hall. Mom and Dad were among them. They looked at Vern expectantly as he unzipped his big black bag and pulled out the Snickers' Cup.

"Shall we put this in the memento cabinet?" He grinned from ear to ear. His smile slowly faded when we didn't respond. "Okay. What gives? I thought winning the prize was a reason to celebrate."

Not that trophy and not that way, I thought.

"Yeah, right. What's so great about beating little kids who were so afraid of getting hurt they let us walk all over them? I'd have been embarrassed if we hadn't won," Alex said.

"Come on, Alex, don't be a poor sport. We won more than one game to get this. Your parents are proud of you." He waved the silver cup in the air.

"But the babies went home crying because it was

the first game they lost. And their parents turned on us if we even mentioned the final game, saying we should be more sensitive to their feelings." Angie's brown eyes smouldered.

Poor Angie, I could guess who she was talking about. Her parents spoiled her little sister — but still, her mom had come to celebrate our victory.

"No one worried about how I, er ... we felt," she continued.

"Exactly. We might not be the world's greatest team but we're not bullies or baby-beaters. We worked hard to get to the finals, just like you said, Coach. It doesn't matter though, because all of River Park wanted their dream team to win. They're acting like we cheated to get that stupid thing." Rosa waved a small hand at the offending object.

There was a murmur of protest from the parents.

"This is, like, *so* not fair, Vern. We belonged there as much as any other team."

"This is brutal. Who's been saying these things?" Vern squatted down to our level.

"Mostly the kids at school. But some of the division nine team's parents, too." Jen twirled a lock of her hair around a finger.

"Just great. Playing in division eight was to give them a chance — not a sure win." Vern shook his head.

"This demented man called me a big fat bully as I left the Spectrum that day. Even though we went easy on the munchkins." Maxie's dark curls bounced as she shook her head.

"Demented is right — the way people are acting. They figured the rugrats were ready for the big leagues. But indoor soccer can be rough. Players get hurt sometimes. It's not our fault they got gun-shy," Alex said.

"The girls are right, you know. The mental and physical maturity of the younger kids should have been taken into consideration before they were put into an unsafe situation. Don't you agree, Aaron?" Mr. Paulsen turned to ask my dad.

Dad nodded.

"We told you that moving an elementary team up was a lousy idea. But, like, nobody would listen. Now do you believe us?" Pam glared at the adults accusingly.

"I'll admit the reaction you've gotten has been unfortunate, but things aren't that simple. The dream teams of the world need places to stretch themselves. At present there's nowhere for them. We're making the best of a bad situation," Angie's mother suggested.

"You're still not listening. Best for whom? Not us average kids. Is anyone even thinking about us? We're not here to provide some underaged super-jocks with a challenge. If you want us to keep playing, stop taking the fun away." As I spoke, my father smiled and nodded.

"Lizzie's right. We can't keep using these kids as sparring partners for junior superstars, or we'll lose them," Dad said.

"Lord knows, that's the last thing we want. The world has enough couch potatoes. Besides, these kids are the bread and butter of the community clubs and it's about time we gave them some respect. But what to do?" Vern rubbed his chin. He stood up and paced a few steps, then smiled. "Time for a city-wide soccer coaches' meeting. The number of soccer players is increasing yearly. Surely we can find a solution. A place for both the elite athletes and the recreational players. Perhaps tiering? I'll need the parents' support. Can I count on you?"

The parents responded with a chorus of yeses, you bets, and uh-huhs.

14 PIECE OF CAKE

"Just come. I need your help," Brock pleaded on the phone.

"But there's no one home," I said.

"You owe me one, Lizzie. I stayed when you needed someone. Just leave a note." He hung up before I could protest.

Leave a note? Ha. We all know what that got me the last time I did that. I phoned Mom on her cell to get permission.

"Okay, what's so important?" I demanded when Brock answered the door.

"You'll find out soon enough." He waved me into the house. "Wait. I'll be right back."

I took off my hiking boots and stepped into the living room. I don't know what I had expected — peeling paint, a shabby couch, threadbare rug? Who knows? But normal wasn't it. This house was well maintained, with a flat-screen TV, video games — all the normal stuff. There were some baseball trophies sitting on a bookshelf. Photos scattered among them told the story. Brock's team had been city champs more than once. His Pythons' jacket didn't come from the thrift store.

When the Brock-o-li came back he was wearing the funny coat and hat. He handed me a bus ticket. "Here, let's go."

He wouldn't tell me where we were going no matter how much I bugged him. All he would say was, "You'll see."

We got off at Meadowood Manor, the local senior citizens' residence. I froze in my tracks.

"I can't go in there."

"Why not?"

Memories of being little and visiting my grandma in a nursing home flooded over me. I could almost smell the antiseptic.

"I hate hospitals," I said.

"Don't worry about it, this isn't a hospital. Come on, it'll be a piece of cake. You'll see." He took my hand and guided me in.

Once inside the doors, I took a deep breath. "I can do this," I said to myself.

The foyer was bright and cheery — all aqua and coral — green plants were scattered among soft uphol-stered chairs. A faint smell of lemon was in the air.

The man at the desk waved to us. "Hey, kid, here for Granny Goss? She's been excited all week."

How sweet, I thought. I followed Brock down the

hall. He was right. It was a piece of cake.

We had barely stepped into the room when a voice said, "So, we finally meet. Let's take a look at you."

The old woman wheeled her chair closer and stared at me. I stared right back.

This wasn't your typical grandma. Wispy curls framed her strong face. The rest of her orange-red hair — dye job, no doubt — was pulled back into a stylish French knot. Her face had hardly a wrinkle, merely exaggerated laugh lines. Her makeup was almost natural looking, all peaches and cream. Perfect brows arched over her bright blue eyes. It was the soft, loose skin on her neck and her frail body that gave away her age. Even though we had never met before, there was something familiar about her.

"Not quite what I expected. Freckle-faced girl next door she's not."

"I never said she had freckles."

"No, no you didn't. But I pictured a teenaged Judy Garland type whenever you told me about her antics."

"Dorothy from *The Wizard of Oz*? — I don't think so," Brock laughed.

I started to get ticked because they were talking about me as if I wasn't there.

"Thanks for introducing me," I said sarcastically.

"Oops, sorry. Lizzie, this is my grandmother, Granny Goss."

I just nodded acknowledgement.

"I've been dying to meet you. You have no idea how often I've asked him to bring you by. Brock's kept me in stitches with his Lizzie stories. Each visit I've look forward to the next instalment. Your escapades have provided much-needed laughter for us at Meadowood Manor." She started to giggle and I remembered the laugh. She was the lady at the winter club. "It cracks me up every time I picture you —"

"I don't know what he's been telling people," I cut her off. "But what I do know is I don't like being laughed at. I came because Brock said he needed my help and I owed him one. I had no idea I was going to be a show-and-tell object. It looks like you two have everything under control, so if you'll excuse me, I'll just head on home now."

I turned to leave. I hoped my face wasn't as red as it usually got when I was angry or embarrassed.

She reached out and grabbed my arm.

"Spunky little thing, isn't she? I like spirited women. We never laughed at you, dear, but with you. The way Brock told it, the joke was usually on him. You gave back as good as he dished out. So please don't go."

I racked my brain to try and figure out when I had ever gotten the best of the Brock-o-li. I gave up. Obviously we saw the same incidents very differently.

"Okay, if I'm going to stay — and I'm not saying I am — I want to know why I am here."

"Like I said, *shweetheart*, we need your help." I hadn't

heard Brock talking like that in a long time.

He picked up a pencil stub from the desk and pretended to take a long drag from a cigarette, then he continued.

"See, I bought these tickets months ago, cupcake. A birthday gift for precious over there." He pointed at Granny Goss with his "cigarette." "Mother promised to take us, but the dame squelched on the deal. She flew off to Edmonton. Claims it's a business trip. Now we're up the creek without a paddle."

"And how am I supposed to help? I can't drive. I'm only twelve, duh."

"Not to worry dear, that's taken care of. I need a female companion just in case I have to go to, you know, the powder room." His grandma whispered the last three words. "I can't always reach the taps or towels."

"Okay, I can handle that," I said.

"Good. Now let's get you in costume."

"Costume? What for? It's not Halloween," I said.

For the first time I noticed that Brock's grandma was wearing a green wool suit. Even old women would have called the outfit old-fashioned, with its padded shoulders and fur-trimmed collar and cuffs. "Suit yourself, but you might feel out of place." His grandma put a funny little hat on her head and adjusted the short net veil that was hanging from it. She got Brock to wrap a fur cape around her shoulders.

I figured we must be going to one of those mystery

thingies or dinner theatres where the audience got involved with the show. You could dress up if you wanted to, but you didn't have to. Mom and Dad went to one once.

"I'll be fine," I said.

Brock wasn't satisfied. "Just in case you change your mind." He grabbed a hat box from the dresser, handed it to me, then wheeled Granny Goss down the hall to the foyer.

"Hey, Miss G., you sure you don't want me to call you a cab?" the deskman called out as we passed.

"You know me, Joe, I prefer Transit Tom's limousine service."

"Limo? Really?" For a minute there I was really excited.

"Well, no, but just as good. Okay, Brock, let's flee this prison." She laughed.

Brock pushed Granny's chair out and headed across the parking lot to the bus shack. Suddenly, I was doubtful.

"How are we going to get her chair on the bus, Brock?" I asked.

"A kneeling bus is on this route today," Granny Goss said.

"A what?" I asked.

"Well, *shweetheart*, it's one of those low-floor numbers with wheelchair access," Brock said.

I must have looked skeptical, for Granny Goss said,

"You won't have to carry anything, I promise. Just come and enjoy the show."

I was eager to see this bus — if it really existed.

The bus pulled up and lowered itself to curb level. When the door opened, a ramp slid forward. Brock pushed Granny onto the bus and fastened the chair with the safety clamps. Jaw dragging, I followed. Isn't technology great? I thought, as I dropped into the sideways seat beside the wheelchair.

★ ★ ★

"Our stop." Brock freed the chair, wheeled it off the bus, and headed for Cinématheque.

"Are we going to a movie? I thought we were going to a play." I laughed.

"Not just any movie, dear, it's the last two films in the 'Best of Bogey Festival' at the theater."

"A Bogeyman Festival? Couldn't you have just rented some movies? I only like scary shows curled up on my own sofa."

"*Shweetheart*, that's Humphrey Bogart, not bogeyman." Brock shook his head and rolled his eyes. "He was a famous actor."

"And that man was meant to be enjoyed on the big screen." Granny Goss fanned her face with her hand.

As we waited in line to buy the popcorn and drinks, I looked at all the other moviegoers. Granny Goss was right. I was the only one dressed normally.

"Why is everyone dressed up to go to a movie?" I whispered.

"The film festival is put on by the Golden Oldies. They're a group of seniors that raise money for sick kids. All the funds from today will be going to set up a home-theater system at the children's hospital. One of the sponsors of the event is a local costume rental company and they offered to donate two dollars to the cause for each person who comes in costume," Granny Goss explained.

"Why didn't you tell me that in the first place, you jerk?" I swatted Brock lightly on the arm.

"I put this getup on so often — whenever I go to visit my Bogey fan, here — it slipped my mind that this time I was doing it for another reason."

I glanced down at the hat box I was carrying. "Get me a cola and buttered popcorn. I'll be right back."

In the ladies washroom I opened the box. A long slim skirt and a small black hat were in it. I pulled the skirt on over my jeans and plopped the hat on my head. It looked ridiculous to me. I shrugged. Oh well, it's for a good cause, I thought. I tried to fold my jacket into the box but it wouldn't fit, so I carried it.

When I got back to the foyer, Brock was just about to pay for our stuff.

"How much do I owe?" I held out some bills.

He waved my money away. "My treat. After all, I

asked you to come."

"You don't have to. It's not like it's a date," I said.

"Don't be too sure about that. Right, Brock?" The old lady smiled and winked.

The Brock-o-li turned beet red and headed for the theater, leaving me to push the wheelchair.

We sat in the back so Granny's chair could be tucked out of the way. After a short lecture about the movies, the lights went down and *The Maltese Falcon* began, followed by *Casablanca*. By the end of the shows, everything about Brock had fallen into place — his funny hat, coat, and strange way of talking — a Humphrey Bogart wannabe. Strange boy, stumbling along in the wrong decade, I thought.

We said our goodbyes to Granny Goss at the front door of Meadowood Manor.

"Thanks for coming, dear. Don't be a stranger." She turned to Brock. "Kid, you sure can pick 'em. This girlfriend's a keeper."

Girlfriend? Where'd she get that idea from? I handed the hat box with the costume to her and followed Brock back to the bus stop.

"You know, you looked cute in that hat, cupcake," Brock said as we waited for the bus.

Just like I thought, the kid saw things very differently than I did. "Right. A regular beauty queen," I mumbled, embarrassed.

"Well, did you enjoy the movies?"

"Yeah. Yeah, I did. I didn't think I could like a black-and-white film." I was glad he'd changed the subject.

"If you ever feel you want some more, come up and join us sometime. I come and visit every Saturday. Sometimes during the week, too. We watch old movies, read old detective mysteries, share some laughs. You'd enjoy it, cupcake."

"I just might. But let's drop the 'cupcake' thing, okay?"

"But, *shweetheart*, how can I? Every time I look at you I see Ingrid Bergman."

The movie star from *Casablanca*? Yeah, right, if I was ten years older and a lot prettier, maybe.

I blushed with pleasure, though. The poor, sweet, mixed-up boy!